Re
OCT 2 0 2012
Ballard Branch

NO LONGER THE PROPERTY
OF THE SEATTLE PUBLIC LIBRARY

D0341612

BUSHMAN LIVES!

BY
DANIEL PINKWATER

ILLUSTRATIONS BY
CALEF BROWN

Houghton Mifflin
Houghton Mifflin Harcourt
Boston   New York   2012

To Jill, the gorilla of my dreams.

Text copyright © 2012 by Daniel Pinkwater
Illustrations copyright © 2012 by Calef Brown

All rights reserved. For information about permission
to reproduce selections from this book, write to
Permissions, Houghton Mifflin Harcourt Publishing Company,
215 Park Avenue South, New York, New York 10003.

Houghton Mifflin is an imprint of
Houghton Mifflin Harcourt Publishing Company.

www.hmhbooks.com

The text of this book is set in Apollo MT.
The illustrations were created in brush and ink.

Library of Congress Cataloging-in-Publication Data
Pinkwater, Daniel Manus, 1941–
Bushman lives! / written by Daniel Pinkwater ; illustrated by Calef Brown.
p. cm.
Summary: In the 1960s, Harold Knishke, a Chicago teenager with a special place
in his heart for Bushman, the famed departed gorilla of the Lincoln Park Zoo,
embarks on a hometown adventure, in a quest to become a great artist
and figure out how he became the object of a famous folk song.

ISBN 978-0-547-38539-6

[1. Coming of age—Fiction. 2. Artists—Fiction. 3. Chicago (Ill.)—History—20th
century—Fiction. 4. Adventure and adventurers—Fiction. 5. Humorous stories.]
I. Brown, Calef, ill. II. Title.

PZ7.P6335Bu 2012

[Fic]—dc23

2011048211

Manufactured in the United States of America
DOC 10 9 8 7 6 5 4 3 2 1
4500375069

CONTENTS

CHAPTER 1

A Goon in My Room

I must have been asleep for an hour or two. I woke up sensing there was someone in my room.

"Geets?"

"Ook ook, Bushman lives," Geets Hildebrand said.

"Ook," I said. I switched the light on.

Geets was sitting cross-legged next to my bed. He had done this before. Sometimes I would wake in the morning and there he would be, sleeping on the rug. I could never get him to tell me how he got in—how he got into a building with a doorman, into a locked elevator area, into our locked apartment, and into my locked bedroom. Had he slipped past the doorman and picked three locks? Had my father, who disliked and mistrusted all my friends, let him in and for some reason agreed not to say anything about it? It was a mystery.

"Drink to Bushman," Geets said. He pulled four bottles of Guinness out of his jacket, and two bananas. This was our ritual. We would drink to Bushman the Gorilla at the Lincoln Park Zoo, and eat bananas, which actually went quite well with the thick, bitter Guinness.

Bushman was a hero to us. Bushman weighed 427 pounds, and was completely ugly, even for a gorilla. He wasn't round and paunchy like most gorillas you see in zoos. He had the build of a weightlifter, a cruel face, white sharp teeth, and these tiny black eyes. I used to get close to the bars when I was a little kid and gaze into those eyes. Bushman would get his chin down to the floor of the cage and gaze back into mine. It felt like we were having a conversation, that I knew what he was thinking. He resented being caged, but he was not mad at anyone. He liked people, especially kids. His keeper would hand him quarts of milk through the bars, and he would politely hand the empties back. Sometimes he would catch mice in his cage and play with them gently.

When Bushman was a baby and a young ape, the keepers would take him out on the lawn to wrestle and pass a football with him. But the day came when Bushman realized he didn't need to go back into the cage if he didn't want to, and it took six keepers three hours to get him there. After that he was never taken outside again.

Bushman knew he was a prisoner, confined through no choice of his own, and he didn't pretend to like it. He remembered that time on the lawn and wanted to get out there again, only this time he would not let them get him back into the Great Ape House. He got along with his keepers, and of course kids. But he didn't express friendliness in some undignified way. He didn't make cute faces or do little tricks to please the crowd like some chimp. He was not a smiley gorilla. He kept his dignity. He'd had a bad break, but he wasn't about to let it break him. Maybe that is why he was the most popular animal in the zoo—there are a lot of people in Chicago who feel the same way. The zoo never made a cartoon version of Bushman to use as an advertising mascot. No politician ever posed for a picture with Bushman or claimed Bushman had endorsed him. Nobody would have believed it.

People who tried to get him to respond, acting like fools in front of his cage, got a look from him that made them shut up and move on. It was clear what that look meant: "Look at yourself and look at me—and tell me who is the superior animal . . . you jerk."

When I was a little kid, Bushman and I would commune, our faces close as we could get them, Bushman playing idly with a piece of celery. He was my friend. All the kids in Chicago felt the same as I did about him. I used to believe that if I got in trouble, if I got surrounded by bullies, somehow Bushman would come and rescue me. I felt that I was a special person because I knew him. A half-million people had visited him one time when he got sick, and years later when he died the whole city mourned.

But he was not dead to Geets and me. He would never be dead. We drank our Guinnesses and ate our bananas. We always did this. We would always do it.

Of course, I really did know how Geets got into my room. I just didn't want to admit it to myself. He had been coming through the window. He had climbed up six floors with four bottles of Guinness and two bananas. Geets Hildebrand was a genius building climber, as well as trees, monuments, streetlights, and statues in the park. I had never seen him go up a building any higher than mine, but there was no reason he could not have climbed higher. It was his nature. If he lived in the Alps or the Himalayas instead of Chicago, he would have scampered up the Matterhorn or Everest before breakfast every day.

Geets's other unusual talent was . . . I guess you'd call it ventriloquism. He could throw his voice. I mean really throw it—a long way. He didn't do words, or make a dummy talk, or anything like that. He had invented sounds, and he could make you think you were hearing them from a long way off. One was a combination of a hum and a thump—that one he could cause to sound like it was coming from the other side of a wall, or a closed door. Then there was the hydrogen beep—that was the sound of hydrogen exploding, which you would swear was happening right behind your head. But his best sound was the dying eagle. This was a chilling scream, maybe a hundred feet up in the air. He would be on a busy sidewalk, say on Michigan Avenue, and he would do the dying eagle. People all around would look up, startled. A complete stranger could be standing right next to Geets when he made that sound, and the guy would look not at Geets but straight up.

The other thing about Geets, not a talent exactly, was the way people reacted to him. He was quiet, and relaxed in his manner—his face always had a sort of tranquil expression. He was tall, and moved slowly.

He wore nondescript clothing—a shirt, baggy slacks, black shoes, stuff he got at the Salvation Army store, always in dull colors, beige, dirty yellow, pale green. Whenever we went into a store, the owner would be pretty sure it was a holdup. Sometimes they called the police. He would do no more than step inside the door and someone would get scared. Cops would stop him on the street and ask him what he was doing.

"Nothing, officer," he would say in a quiet voice. "I'm just minding my own business."

We had just finished our junior years at different high schools and were free for the summer. He went to Tesla Tech, the all-boys technical high school. It was all shop, and math, and engineering. I went to Riverview, possibly the most boring high school on the planet. It had no distinguishing characteristics, unless you count that nobody liked being there, neither students nor teachers, and everybody was mildly depressed.

If there was a happy person at Riverview, it would have had to be me. This was because I held the positions of captain of the hall guards, and chief fire marshal, which meant I had freedom of movement—I could be anywhere in the building anytime I wanted, could get up and leave a class, saying it was fire marshal business, and of course I could leave the building, go across the street, and have a Coke with no one to say me nay.

The captain of the hall guards was in charge of all the kids who sat at little desks at the ends of hallways and asked people who were loose during class time for their hall passes, signed by teachers. I have no idea what they were supposed to do if someone didn't have a pass, and I never found out what the chief fire marshal was supposed to do—except I got advance notice of fire drills, had a little map showing where all the fire exits were, and had a full set of keys to the school.

This is how I got to be such an important official: When I was a freshman, my mother said to me, "I met the nicest woman in the market. Her son is a senior at Riverview, and he is coming to see you this afternoon."

"What? Are you picking friends for me? This is embarrassing," I told my mother.

"Well, be nice to him. He is a senior, and you are just starting at the school, and it is very nice of him to come and visit you."

A little while later, this kid appeared in my room. He was a kid, but looked more like an adult. He had a better haircut than any kid, and he was wearing a great-looking sport jacket with a Nixon button in the lapel—he looked somehow cleaner than me. He had a firm handshake and a very smooth hand.

"My name is Ralph Noble," the kid said.

I mumbled. "Harold Knishke."

"The reason I wanted to meet you," Ralph Noble said, "is that your mother told my mother you might be willing to support me in my run for student body president. Can I count on your vote?"

"You're running for student body president?"

"Look, when people meet me, they like me. You like me, don't you?"

"Well . . . sure," I said. He was sort of likable in a scary, artificial way.

"So how about it? Will you back me for student body president?"

"You can count on me," I said.

"Great. My campaign people will be in touch."

"Bushman lives," I said.

"Huh?" he said.

There was an assembly, and all the candidates made speeches. Ralph's speech was lousy. The other speeches were lousy too, but his was the lousiest. He did not get elected.

And that was all there was to it—I thought. But a few days later, this kid with remarkably thick glasses came up to me.

"My name is Bobby Noonan," the kid said. His glasses made his eyes look like brown fish swimming in bowls. "Our candidate lost, but your work on the campaign is appreciated, and here is your reward."

Bobby Noonan handed me a rectangular piece of felt—it was an armband, with the letters LT/HG stitched on it.

"You are now a lieutenant of the hall guards. One period a day, you are to patrol the halls, making sure the hall guards are at their posts and asking people to show their passes. You are on duty fifth period, and if you want to go outside for a smoke or anything, feel free, but don't be obvious about it."

Bobby Noonan belonged to the sight-saving class. This was a special room for kids who were nearly blind, and they had large-print books, better lighting than the other classrooms, and projectors and things. Also, by some kind of coincidence, most of these kids were the children of guys who were active in Chicago politics, so they knew how things were done. And they were Ralph Noble's brain trust and campaign managers.

I don't think I ever had another conversation with Ralph Noble, or Bobby Noonan, but as time passed and people graduated, I got regular promotions in the hall guards, and at some point was informed that I was a fire marshal, and I finally became the top man in both organizations—never taking any of it seriously or having a clue what any of it meant other than a license to cut classes, which is all that made my life at the school tolerable.

Geets had pulled the bedspread off my bed, wrapped himself in it, curled up on my rug, and gone to sleep. I drifted off too, feeling cozy with the two Guinnesses in me.

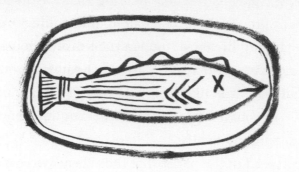

CHAPTER 2

Breakfast with the Knishkes

"So, Harold, I see your weird friend got in again last night," my father said at breakfast.

"What are your plans for the summer?" my mother asked Geets.

"I'm thinking of joining the navy, Mrs. Knishke," Geets said.

"You'll look cute in your uniform, Geets, dear," my mother said.

"It's a good idea. They'll make a man of you," my father said.

"Have another kipper, Geets, darling," my mother said.

"Yum, kipper!" Geets said.

"*Gut Yontiff,*" my father said.

A kipper is a whole herring that has been split from tail to head, gutted, salted, and cold-smoked. It is a standard breakfast food in the Knishke household. If you have never tried a kipper, I suggest you keep it that way. It is like eating an oily fish made of rubber. I, of course, am used to them. English people eat them. And my family.

"I read in the paper that those bears were making a disturbance in the park again," my mother said.

"Wolves, not bears," my father said. "The only bears in Chicago play football."

My parents read this paper that is thirty-two pages long and comes out once a week. It has stories the regular papers don't carry—like about wolves in Lincoln Park. I love my parents, and accept them for the good kipper-eating people they are. Good, but completely insane. Just as an example, my father will not look at reruns on television, even if he did not see the program the first time.

"I did not pay three hundred and seventy-nine dollars for this fine television set to look at old shows," he says.

And although we live in a high-rise apartment building, my mother refused to have an apartment on one of the upper floors, where we would have had a spectacular view. She said it would be too dangerous should any of us happen to fall out a window. So she picked an apartment on the sixth floor, even though I pointed out that a fall from that high would be just as fatal. Not to mention adults almost never accidentally fall out of windows.

Geets was still breakfasting with my parents when I left for my music lesson.

CHAPTER 3

A Tutor Who Tooted the Flute

Every Saturday I took the bus downtown to take a flute lesson with Emil Pfiff in the Fine Arts Building, right on Michigan Avenue across from Grant Park. The Fine Arts Building is about seventy-five years old, built in 1885 for people like me to take music lessons in. Also it has studios for painters and architects and people like that, a theater—the Studebaker—downstairs, and the place is full of murals, and stained-glass windows, and everywhere you look there are carvings and decorations in the art nouveau style, which is a combination of fake medieval and wiggly-looking vegetables. Over the doorway as you enter are bronze letters that read ALL PASSES—ART ALONE ENDURES, and going up in the old-fashioned elevator, you hear opera singers howling, and people sawing away on cellos—also there is the aroma of cabbage cooking and pork chops, because some of the music teachers and artists live in their little offices and studios to save on rent.

Emil Pfiff is an old German guy with white hair and a mustache. He's played second flute in the Chicago Symphony Orchestra for about a hundred years, and when he's not doing that he sits in this little room in the Fine Arts Building, tutoring tooters to toot.

"*Ach, Himmel,*" Pfiff said. "It's you again."

"It's me every Saturday at this time, Mr. Pfiff," I said.

"Ja, and vhat I vant to know is vhy?"

"Vhy? I mean, why? To take my lesson," I said.

"Und you neffer think maybe to quit?"

"Why should I think of that? Why should I quit?"

"Look, Knabe, mein boy, you are a nice boy, but musically you shtink. Haff you never thought about maybe you haff no talent vhatsoever?"

"Do you think I have no talent whatsoever?"

"*Mein Gott!* Ve haff been vorking on 'O Haupt voll Blut und Wunden,' specially arranged for flute shtoodent, for a year already! Und no progress— none! Vhy did you take up the instrument in the first place?"

The reason I had taken up the flute in the first place was that it was the smallest instrument and easy to carry around. And the reason I took up an instrument at all was so I could be in the Riverview High School band, which meant that in addition to the two periods a day I spent doing my duty as an officer of the hall guards, there was a period of band, which was one less period of sitting in class. Classes at Riverview were hard to take, and best kept to a minimum. I was just barely good enough to hold down fourth chair in the flute section. Delores Rhinebeck, Sue Krantz, and Jean Blanc, the rest of the flute section, were all better than me, and older than me, and covered for me. I was in love with all three of them, especially their breasts. But Delores, Sue, and Jean, and their breasts, had all just graduated, and there was going to be some kind of horrible reckoning when school started in September and Captain Walz, the band teacher, could actually hear me.

"Look, I make you a proposition," Pfiff said. "Vhat about you just don't come back anymore?"

"You want me to quit?"

"Ja, just fade away. You are giving me migraine every Saturday. Also I vill buy that flute off you for fifty bucks. I don't like to think of it in your hands."

I had to admit, it was a good deal. The flute had only cost sixty-five to begin with.

"Can I keep the case?" I asked Mr. Pfiff.

"Ach, so! I am reading your mind. Ja, you may keep the case, but if your father asks me, I tell everything."

This is how I was rationalizing the deal: Obviously, the money was wasted anyway. I could continue to collect the three-fifty a week that had paid for the music lessons up to now. I told myself that now that I wasn't giving it to Pfiff, I would spend it on other forms of education or self-improvement. I could carry the flute case around with me—it could be useful for transporting small objects or as a weapon of self-defense. My parents would not notice that I was not practicing, since I never did anyway. And I didn't have to make up my mind right away—if I decided not to be dishonest, I could give my father the fifty and tell him Pfiff had fired me from being his student. Also, not having an instrument would solve my problem with Captain Walz in the fall.

Emil Pfiff was smiling a beautiful smile. "Gott, I feel so relieved," he said. "I vill neffer have to listen to your playing again. Do not take it as a judgment that you cannot make music if your life depended. I am sure there are many things you can do . . . just this is not one. You ver not thinking you vould grow up to be Mozart, ver you?"

"Who?"

"Go, mein boy. It is a beautiful day. Go and enjoy it."

"Bushman lives," I said

"Gesundheit," Emil Pfiff said.

CHAPTER 4

Ars Longa Vita Brevis

Two minutes later, I was on the other side of Michigan Avenue, heading in the direction of the Art Institute, with an empty flute case and free as a wild gorilla.

THE ART INSTITUTE OF CHICAGO, it said in letters carved into the stone up near the top. Big, official-looking building with wide steps going up to it, and a couple of green lions on either side. I had been there a couple of times on school trips. I was standing there, looking at it, and thinking about how there was nothing I had to do. I owned my own life. I could go wherever I wanted to go.

I could go in there. I could go into the Art Institute, look around, see the art. The last time, I was with a gang of seventh-graders and we moved along in a group and got lectured at. I hesitated with one foot on the bottom step.

"Going inside, 'bo?" someone said.

It was a chick. Little, sort of chubby chick. She was sitting next to one of the green lions. She had little squinty black glasses, a black raincoat, and multicolored knee socks.

"I thought I might," I said.

"Well, do it already," the chick said. "Go look at a painting called *Excavation* by Willem de Kooning."

"*Excavation*?"

"That's what I said. Check it out. It does things."

"Okay, I will," I said.

"Do so," the chick said.

"*Excavation*."

"It's upstairs. You can't miss it."

I have to mention that this was possibly the longest conversation I had ever had with a girl outside of school. I felt I was handling it fairly well, and I didn't want to hang around and blow it.

"Thanks," I said.

"Don't mention it, mister."

I went up the stairs and into the museum.

The painting was a complete disappointment.

At first. It looked like . . . nothing. There was a lot of dirty white, with sketchy black lines, and here and there a little bit of color peeking out. It was huge. I wondered what the chick with the goggles thought was so good about it. I stood gazing at it, trying to see if maybe it was of something, like those puzzles in the back of the Sunday funnies where it's a tree and the caption says, "How many squirrels can you find in the tree?" If you look for a while, you see there are squirrels green on green, hidden in the tree. Maybe it was something like that. She said it did things.

And then . . . it started to do things. Yes, indeed, it did things. It started to wiggle or vibrate— or maybe I was wiggling and vibrating. I felt myself being pulled into the painting, by the eyeballs. This is hard to explain, but I was able to get behind the dirty white parts . . . well, not me, not physically me, but my mind. My mind went into the painting, and it was like some crazy board game. I got taken this way and that, and the colors, the reds and blues and yellows, were moving, sometimes where I couldn't see, and then they'd pop out and show themselves. And I was moving with them. It was like listening to music with my eyes. It was fantastic fun. It was exciting— and at the same time it was a little scary, because an inanimate thing, paint on a big piece of canvas, was playing with me as though it were alive.

And then the painting spat me out. Or maybe I pulled out, because it was just too weird and unexpected. I felt excited and strange, and I noticed my heart was beating a little fast. I had a funny taste in my mouth too. I didn't want to stay in the museum any more—that was enough for the first time.

I went out to see if the chick in the raincoat was still there.

She wasn't, but what was there was Michigan Avenue, which had been there in the first place, and which I had seen hundreds and hundreds of times— only I had not seen it like I was seeing it now. The sky was blue, as it often was, only this time it was not only blue, but it was . . . thick. It had a texture. If I could have reached up and taken a piece of sky between my thumb and finger, I could have felt it. The buildings were stone, and brown, and bluish gray, and tall— like always—only I felt they were somehow curving, huddling together, and arching out over the street. And the cars! The cars were all these amazing colors, moving along like big beetles, metallic and rounded, and shiny. I could see the air too. It was all amazing. Something had happened to my eyes, or my brain, while I was away inside the painting. By the time I had gotten back inside myself, all my seeing settings had been changed.

I sat down next to the lion, where the chick had been sitting, and waited to get used to it. I guessed that was what she had been doing. After a while, I did sort of adjust, though everything continued to look very good to me, and I felt oddly happy and buzzy.

CHAPTER 5

Walking Home

I was in no hurry. I decided to walk all the way home. I felt like looking around with my eyes all tuned up after the experience in the museum. It was a bright day, a little on the cool side, and perfect for walking and exploring.

I crossed Michigan Avenue and entered the deep canyons of the Loop. It was always a little darker among the tall buildings, and breezy and busy. I was in no hurry—I went in and out of lobbies of various buildings, looked at things in store windows, sniffed the cooking smells outside restaurants, and observed the people, all of whom were walking fast, as though they knew where they were going.

I got all the way to the west side of the Loop,

hooked a right, crossed the Chicago River, and started in the direction of my neighborhood. Once I was across the river, the buildings were smaller and more sunlight hit the street. The stores were less fancy, ranging to crummy, and some had dusty windows. There were a few three- and four-story apartment houses in between commercial buildings. The traffic wasn't as heavy, and the people weren't as thick on the sidewalk. It was more than fifty blocks to our apartment building, at least six miles. I could do it in two hours, if I walked steadily, but strolling, making stops, and pausing for a fast lunch, I could stretch it out to three or four hours—that is what I decided to do.

I came upon a little bookstore. Christmas Royal Books. Wait a minute! I knew this store—only I didn't know it was where it was now. Christmas Royal's bookstore was formerly on Broadway, a few blocks from my house. Then, one day it wasn't there anymore. Obviously he had moved and this was his new location. I went in, and sure enough, there he was, Christmas Royal, the skinniest man in Chicago. When I say that Christmas Royal was skinny, I mean he was like a skeleton. In addition to being skinny, he was tall, had red hair he wore in a spiky crewcut, and also had the thickest glasses anyone had ever seen. He also had a long pointy nose.

"Well, well, looky here," Christmas Royal said. "Harold Knishke, as I live and breathe. White Fang! Front!"

White Fang was Christmas Royal's dog, a boxer, and he knew more tricks than Lassie. The dog appeared from the back of the store, bounded over the counter, and sat facing Christmas Royal.

"Watch him, Fang," Christmas Royal said. "It's Harold Knishke, the well-known book thief."

White Fang wheeled around and gave me the serious eyeball.

"Mr. Royal, I have never stolen a book!" I said.

"We'll just keep it that way," Christmas Royal said. "White Fang, if he tries to put anything under his coat, bite him, but do not kill him." To me he said, "You may move around normally, but keep your hands in plain sight. What brings you down this way, Harold?"

"Just taking the long way home," I said.

"Harold, admit it, you've been coming into the other store for years, trying to pilfer comic books . . ."

"I never!"

"And now you've tracked me down in my new location to rob me blind and try to put me out of business. Otherwise, why would you even enter a bookstore? You are a lout without culture."

"On the contrary," I said. "In fact, just today I went into the Art Institute and looked at a painting."

"Yes. I understand that's where they keep the paintings," Christmas Royal said. "Are you planning a career as an art thief?"

"It was pretty good, the painting."

"I'm glad for you. Be sure to send the artist a fan letter." Christmas Royal settled back in his chair and began reading a copy of the *Hobo News.*

"Well, I guess I'll be going," I said.

"Tell you what," Christmas Royal said. "To commemorate your coming into my new store for the first time, I am going to give you a free book, with the cover torn off. Here."

Christmas Royal handed me a crummy-looking paperback with the cover torn off. The title page read, *Modern Art, An Invention of the Devil? by Rev. Nathan DuNord.*

"Thanks, Mr. Royal," I said. "Bushman lives."

"Get lost, Harold," Christmas Royal said.

CHAPTER 6

Fame Game

I patted White Fang on the head, then went outside to resume my walk. After a while, I came upon the E. J. Sperry Thought Factory. This was a two-story house on a quiet corner. It had a sort of courtyard in front, and an iron fence.

Attached to the fence was the sign that said E. J. SPERRY THOUGHT FACTORY and a couple of cork bulletin boards. Pinned to the bulletin boards were little scraps of paper of various colors and sizes, with things written on them in a variety of handwriting and with different colors of ink. The things written ranged from tight little paragraphs to single words, phrases, mathematical equations—I presumed these were the thoughts. I didn't know if I was supposed to leave one, take one, or just read them. There were no instructions telling how the E. J. Sperry Thought Factory worked, or what it was supposed to be.

I read some of the messages on the slips of paper. $E=mc^2$. *Kilroy was here. I think, therefore I am. Nov Shmoz Ka-pop. Shlermie, where are you? I'd rather have a bottle in front of me than a frontal lobotomy. Ontogeny recapitulates phylogeny. I am hungry. Free Jomo Kenyatta. Ban the Bomb. For a good time call KLondike-5-6700.* Apparently, Geets Hildebrand had been here, or someone who thought along the same lines—one of the notes read, *Bushman lives.* I took out my pen, and wrote *I agree* on the same paper.

I was about to move on when I noticed another message. It had my name in it! It said, *Harold Knishke lives.* What the?? It wasn't in the same handwriting as the *Bushman lives* message. I checked in case it was Geets fooling around, which would have been impressive, since how was he to know I would be reading that bulletin board? But it was a different hand, different ink, different paper. Of course, the note could have referred to another Harold Knishke, but there wasn't another one as far as I knew. My family were the only Knishkes in the Chicago phone book.

I sort of liked that someone had written my name, was thinking about me. This was the most famous I had ever been. All through school, and high school, most people, except for my few friends, didn't know my name, and here someone had posted it in a thought at the E. J. Sperry Thought Factory, whatever that was. I considered taking the little piece of paper with me, but then I would stop being famous. I wrote *I certainly do* underneath and pinned it back on the bulletin board.

CHAPTER 7

Bughouse Square

Finding my name pinned to the bulletin board had surprised me, and confused me. It caused a kind of dizzy, unreal feeling, a little bit like the way the painting had made me feel. My emotions had been getting a workout all morning. I walked along, taking in all the colors and textures and feeling the air against my skin, when I saw something rich and strange. It was Bughouse Square in full cry right in the middle of the day!

Bughouse Square is what everyone calls Washington Square Park, the oldest park in Chicago. I doubt that many people even know its real name. It is not big—maybe a block square, across the street from the Newberry Library, of which I have seen the inside—before being kicked out, because high school and college undergraduate students are not allowed. It is a reference library—you can't check books out, but have to sit and read them within the building— and I am told you can ask for just about anything, original Shakespeare folios, ancient manuscripts, ul- tra-rare books worth thousands of dollars, and they will just bring them to you at your little table. And you can leave books and notes on the table and they will be there waiting for you the next day. And it is completely quiet in the Newberry Library. They say you could die and nobody would notice. Scholars and professors and writers use the library, also bums who like to read. I would like to go in and read books, and I have wondered if I would be allowed in if I quit high school.

It's just the opposite in Bughouse Square. This is the place where anybody at all can stand up and make a speech, or have a debate, or argue with a whole crowd of people. Also, people get up and sing, or play instruments, or dance, rave and scream—any- thing goes, as long as you keep your clothes on. There is also grass and trees, and benches, like any park, and people taking a walk, or feeding pigeons, and old guys playing chess.

Most of the action is at night, and on a summer evening, the place is full of people, with maybe five or six speakers carrying on in different parts of the park, and other speakers waiting for them to finish so they can take a turn. Bughouse Square audiences are not polite. They interrupt, argue, holler, and make personal comments—speaking there is a blood sport. It takes nerve. Many a student from the Moody Bible Institute not far away has reconsidered becoming a preacher after being heckled by that crowd.

Here it was, the middle of a spring morning, and the park was doing a fair amount of business. There was a guy hollering about Jesus to two or three old ladies, and a little way off someone was pushing vegetarianism to a half-dozen people who were hooting and cracking jokes. The biggest crowd was listening to a stocky guy in an army cap who was getting red in the face and punching the air with his fist. I wandered closer so I could hear what he was saying.

"Suckers! Dummies! Stooges! Cannon fodder! Patsys! That's you!" the guy shouted. "You're the fat, happy, stupid, hard-working, nonthinking, hot-dog eating, sleepwalking *Boobus americanus,* sheep for the slaughter! You're consumers, shoppers, renters, soldiers, workers, voters, and you haven't got a clue."

This guy was good. He was abusing the heck out of the crowd, and they were clustering closer to get more of it. Nobody was heckling him—he was heckling them. I moved in closer myself.

"Do you realize that you are owned body and soul by oligarchs? Rich guys on the Gold Coast, or up in the suburbs, are driving Cadillacs, hitting golf balls, eating prime rib, and collecting art on your sweat, and every once in a while they maximize profits by dressing you up in uniforms and sending you somewhere to get your asses shot off—and away you march because some worthless hypocrite in a pulpit told you that God wants you to do it, or some crook in an expensive suit told you that you are protecting the American Way. You want to know how come they can do it? You want to know how they work the swindle?"

"Yeah!" people in the crowd shouted. "How do they do it? Those rich bastards!"

"It's easy. They have a system. It's a system for making everybody into zombies who will do what they're told. You know what it's called?"

"What? What's it called?"

"It's called . . . education," the guy said. "They start working on you in kindygarten. They teach you how to behave, and they get you used to turning off your brain by making things so unbearable that you can't stand the pain. You! Young man!"

He was pointing at me. "Me?" I said.

"Yes, you. Come up here."

"You want me to come up there?"

"Just step up here. I want these fine people to see you." He held out his hand. I stepped up onto the little concrete wall, about a foot high, where he was standing. "What's your name, sonny?"

"Harold," I told him.

"You and I have never met before, is that correct?"

"Correct," I said.

"And I am assuming you attend some high school."

"Correct," I said. I was looking out at the crowd, which was sixty or seventy people by this time.

"Now, ladies and gentlemen, I ask you to regard Harold here. He is a fine young man, appears to be healthy, reasonably strong. You are not congenitally feeble-minded, are you, Harold?"

"Not to my knowledge," I said.

"Of normal intelligence. But observe the lack of luster in the eyes, ladies and gentlemen, the passive stance, the slack-jawed expression. Harold, while the fires of youth still burn within him, and while he has not yet been beaten into a lump of obedient human clay, is most probably doomed."

"The poor kid! He's doomed!" people in the crowd shouted.

"Harold, what is the first word that comes to mind when I ask you to describe your experience in the public school system?"

"Well . . . it's . . . boring," I said.

"Boring. Exactly. And Harold, what would any normal person do when confronted by something that is certain to be boring?"

"Avoid it?" I said.

"Precisely. And if you physically can't avoid it, can't get away from it, you learn to settle into yourself quietly, and wait for it to go away. And that is what we teach Harold in school. Sit still, turn off the brain, wait for the end of the day, then stumble out into the sunlight, brain slowly dying because it hasn't been fed anything, and get a smoke, a Coke, a beer, or some other drug. Harold, do you hate high school?"

"Yeah! I hate it!" I said.

"Has it done you the least good?"

"High school has not done me the least good," I said. I was actually starting to enjoy being up there with the guy in the soldier hat.

"Has it ever occurred to you that it is set up the

way it is on purpose? How do you feel about the idea that the whole purpose of sending you to school has been to break your spirit and make you docile?"

"It makes me feel better about the whole thing," I said.

"It does?" Soldier hat was not expecting this answer. I think he wanted me to say I was mad.

"Sure. Because if someone is doing it deliberately, then they are merely evil, and if I have to pick, I'd rather deal with evil people than stupid ones. You can defeat or escape from evil people, but if the whole system is stupid, top to bottom, then you're just sunk."

"That's an interesting point of view, Harold," the guy in the overseas cap said. "Is there something you plan to do, should you survive the school system?"

I don't know why I said it—I certainly had never thought about it before. What I said was "I'm going to try to be some kind of artist."

"Thanks, Harold. You may step down now. I want to explain to these people about capitalism."

I shook hands with the guy and waved to the crowd. "Bushman lives," I said.

"Bushman lives!" they hollered back.

CHAPTER 8

Heiss Hunden

I wandered away from Bughouse Square, and as I wandered, I wondered if I really could be some kind of artist, and if so, what kind?

My first pick would be to be one of these guys who makes up songs and picks a guitar—but the fact that I had been fired by my music teacher that very morning suggested I might do better to pick something other . . . than a guitar. Writing poetry would not involve any particular expense—a notebook and a ballpoint would be all I'd need—but then I had never made up a poem and didn't find them all that fascinating in English class. Writing stories or books might be better, but there was something pathetic about being a guy who sits and does that all day. I didn't know very much about doing paintings, or making sculpture, but I had enjoyed both in kindergarten and first grade. I was still getting a buzz from the painting I had seen in the Art Institute. It would be pretty neat to know how to make something like that.

I could have thought more, but it was getting harder to think, and I realized why—I was hungry. My morning kippers had worn off. I needed to seek food.

I looked around for a hot dog stand. Here is one of the great things about Chicago—if you have between thirty-five cents and a half-dollar, you can get first-class nutrition practically anywhere. There are hot dog stands all over, and the standard Chicago hot dog comes with everything you need to sustain life . . . until the bright green pickle relish catches up with you and you die.

Some say there is a finite number of hot dogs you can eat before they turn fatal, but the number is different for different people and nobody knows what it is. In addition to the bright green relish, you get the actual sausage made in a factory on Damen Avenue, a bun with poppyseeds, yellow mustard, chopped onion, two wedges of tomato, a kosher pickle spear, celery salt, and two small but powerful peppers called sport peppers. There is a school of thought that believes it is the sport peppers that will kill you in the end, but others believe the peppers neutralize the relish and stave off death. It is a serious breach of etiquette to put catsup on a Chicago hot dog, and some hot dog stands don't offer it. Other places have little packets of catsup, but they tell you to take your hot dog outside before putting it on.

Eating a Chicago hot dog requires skill—it takes practice to minimize how much stuff drips and squirts onto you. Serious gluttons favor sport shirts with busy patterns in colors including bright yellow and dark blotches so the mustard and grease won't show. Really nice ones have images of the little peppers and hunks of tomato.

There was a hot dog stand in the middle of the block. HEISS HUNDEN was written on the awning. I was pretty sure that was German for *hot dogs*. It was a small and dingy place—not one of the citywide chains with bright yellow antibug florescent lights and maybe a giant weenie statue on top. I went in and ordered a regular. I watched the fat, hairy, sweaty guy in the white paper cap and dirty apron assemble it, paid my fifty cents, and turned to eat it at the stainless-steel shelf while looking out the plate-glass window.

It was okay. I experienced the snap as my teeth went though the skin of the hot dog, and I felt the spurt of hot grease. Then there was the strange chemical sensation in the nose—from the relish. I munched contentedly, feeling a kind of bliss as my body began to absorb the salt and fat and the odd vitamin and mineral.

And that is when I decided that yes, I was going to be an artist. All I had to do was find out how to be one. Yes I said yes I will Yes.

CHAPTER 9

Old Town

On October 8, 1871, Chicago caught fire. Four square miles burned to the ground, and as many as three hundred people died. The story everyone knows is that a cow belonging to a Mrs. O'Leary kicked over a kerosene lantern that caught the barn on fire and started the whole thing.

The story not everyone knows, but I do because Christmas Royal showed me in a book, is that at the same time as the Great Chicago Fire, the town of Peshtigo, Wisconsin, 250 miles to the north, burned up with a bunch of other little towns and a million and a half acres of forest, also about 2,500 people, making it the deadliest fire in American history. It didn't get as much publicity as the Chicago fire because it was little towns and not a famous big city.

And, also at the same time, the town of Holland, Michigan, on the other side of the lake, burned to the ground too! A hundred miles north of that, Manistee, Michigan, also lit up. Also Port Huron, Michigan, and a whole lot of territory around it. That was called the Great Michigan Fire.

Those are a lot of big fires to happen at the same time in the Upper Midwest. On the next day, October 9, there was a big fire that destroyed the downtown area of Urbana, Illinois, 140 miles south of Chicago. Christmas Royal's book put forth the theory that the fires were started by a meteor shower. This makes more sense to me than a cow kicking over a lantern. An evil plot involving a bunch of pyromaniacs would make more sense too. The newspaper writer who blamed it on the cow later admitted he'd made that story up.

Anyway, the whole place burned down and the people of Chicago set right about building it all over again. The first load of lumber arrived while the last burning house was still smoking, and the city was re-built, and re-rebuilt, complete with skyscrapers and lots of fancy architecture.

But this one neighborhood—which was burned

flat, except for a tiny handful of buildings that some-how escaped—has some interesting features. There are little cottages, and shanties, and shacks, which must go back to right after the fire. Some of them look as though they were nailed together with whatever wood was at hand. Some of them have little gardens around them. They are in among bigger, more normal-looking houses of different styles and ages, and also brick two, and three-story apartment houses, also ex-perimental-looking houses with a lot of artistic carv-ing and decoration on them, and some big apartment houses and stores. There are some streets with big fancy mansions behind iron gates, with towers and turrets, and stone ornamentation, at least one block on which somebody pried up the regular city side-walks and replaced them with inlaid patterns of glass and ceramic bits.

It's as though the whole neighborhood, which is fairly large, is made up of samples of anything any-one could think of, starting in 1871, right after the fire, and up to the present. The people you see in the streets show as much variety as the buildings—guys in turbans, also derby hats, women wearing dresses that look like tablecloths, or hats with feathers, beat-niks in sandals and beards, people wearing weird metallic fabrics. It's the artistic district and there are places that sell paintings, and you can see paintings and sculptures if you peek into windows. It's an excellent neighborhood to walk around in.

On Potawatomie Street there was this house. It was an old frame house three stories high with a set of stairs leading up to the front door, which was on the second floor. Stairs with handrails made of iron pipe. There was a little garden in front, with a low iron fence. Chimney on top. Windows. And here is the thing about this house—it was white. I mean it was white all over. The glass in the windows was white. The stairs were white. The iron fence in front was white, and the stuff in the garden, all dead, was white.

Not just white, this house was, but chalky, deadly white white. And there were these two old people. I figured old because they were small, and because of the way they moved. You couldn't see any part of them—they were totally swathed in clothing, with heads wrapped in cloth, scarves around their faces, sunglasses, gloves, rags wrapped around their feet. They looked like moving scarecrows. Each of them had a pail of whitewash and a brush, and they moved around, stooped and slow, painting white over the white. I could see that coats of whitewash had built up so the details of the house—the windowsills, the fence, the handrails on the steps—were starting to lose definition and turn soft and gloppy. They had evidently been painting it for a long time. I watched them as they moved around slowly and apparently aimlessly, like bees, dabbing with their brushes.

As eerie and scary as this scene was, the guy on the corner and across the street was eerier and scarier. He could have been Emil Pfiff's insane brother, with the white mustache and the little gold-framed eyeglasses. This guy was standing in front of a brick apartment house, watching the whitewashers with evident pleasure. He had a glass of beer, one of those tall pilsner glasses, from which he took sips. He was smiling, showing tiny teeth, and he was wearing a white apron with bloodstains on it. Either this guy was a butcher—only there wasn't a butcher shop—or he was chopping up bodies or performing operations in his apartment.

I don't have to say that there was an air of unreality about all this. I noticed that when you are seeing something this weird, or surprising, things seem to go silent, as though someone has turned the volume down. It had been like that when I came out of the Art Institute after looking at the painting, and it was like that now. So it was without a soundtrack that I noticed one more thing that made me question whether I had just gone crazy, and that was a full-grown mountain gorilla lurching up Potawatomie Street in my direction.

CHAPTER 10

It's (Not) Alive!

I began to hear the wheels squeaking at the same time I realized the gorilla was not alive, but stuffed and mounted on a piece of plywood with four casters in the corners. A kid was pushing it along the street and having a hard time controlling the direction in which it rolled. This accounted for the realistic gorilla-like gait I had observed.

As the kid and the gorilla approached the corner, one of them spoke to me. It was the kid.

"Care to give me a hand with this?" he asked.

"Sure," I said.

I helped him get the gorilla down the curb, across the street, and up onto the sidewalk. It wasn't that heavy, just awkward. Obviously stuffed gorillas are stuffed with lighter stuff than live gorillas are stuffed with.

"Bring it right in, boys," the guy in the apron said. Of course! He must be a taxidermist! That would explain the bloodstains without it being a horror movie. Only, closer up, I noticed not all the stains were red. Some were blue, some were yellow.

We wrestled the gorilla into the door of the apartment house, and down some stairs into the basement.

It was a big room, set up like a classroom or a lab, with lots of tilt-top tables and stools, and a few easels. At one end was a platform, like a little stage, and the kid and I managed to get the gorilla up onto it. The gorilla was dusty and shedding. I spat out some gorilla hair and wiped some more off my face.

"Thanks for the help," the kid said. He was pretty ugly, a macrocephalic type, with a tall forehead, and bunched together toward the bottom of his face a pair of little pig eyes, a button nose, and a tiny mouth. His hair was combed into a pompador that added another two or three inches to his dome. He looked like a thug, and at the same time something on the cover of a science-fiction paperback. "Here," he said. He held out a half-dollar.

"You don't have to tip me," I said.

"You helped. You want these?" he offered me a pack of Picayune cigarettes.

"No thanks. I don't smoke cigarettes, and if I did I wouldn't smoke those."

"Well, I can get you into the class. Do you want to draw?"

"Draw?"

The kid held out his hand. "I'm Billy Zwieback. Arnold Zwieback, the guy in the apron, is my father. This is his drawing class. If I ask him, you can stay and draw. Ordinarily it would cost you three dollars and fifty cents."

"Draw the gorilla?"

"There'll be a model, too," Billy Zwieback said. "I can lend you a sketchbook and some stuff to draw with."

"Yeah, I'd like to draw. My name is Harold Knishke."

"Okay," Billy said. "I'll fix it up with my dad."

"By the way, what's with the whitewashers across the street?" I asked.

"Leave them alone," Billy Zwieback said. "If you get close to them, they'll hiss at you."

"Are they loonies or what?"

"Loonies, definitely."

CHAPTER 11

Drawing from Life

The art students drifted in. They were all older than me, and looked sort of depressed. Among them was the chick who had spoken with me on the steps of the Art Institute. She didn't appear to recognize me. I considered going over and greeting her, but she had this morose expression, as though somebody had just died. They all looked like that, and most of them had on black clothing. They sat on the stools and began adjusting their little drawing tables and unpacking their drawing materials.

After a while, the model came in. She had a sort of flat expression, bored to death looking, and straight hair that was between brown and blond. She was wearing a bathrobe. She stepped up onto the platform with the gorilla, untied the belt of her robe, sort of shrugged it off, and tossed it onto a chair. I had a moment of unreality. She was naked. She was completely bare. I had never seen a naked female before, and therefore it was interesting—but in itself, not. She was on the old side, maybe in her late twenties, and skinny, stringy, wobbly, and saggy all at once. Later, during the break, when all the art students were standing on the corner smoking cigarettes, I heard them talking about her. They said she had a complicated body and was hard to draw, therefore a good model. Apparently cute is easier to draw.

"Five-minute poses," Arnold Zwieback said.

The model froze, one hand on the gorilla's shoulder, and the drawers began to draw. I tried to draw the model and the gorilla too.

It took about thirty seconds for the discomfort of there being a naked woman in the room to wear off, and the discomfort of not being able to get the thick pencil Billy Zwieback had loaned me to do what I wanted to set in. Billy had also given me a big blue eraser, and I used it a lot.

Arnold Zwieback walked around among the drawing tables, smoking a cigar. He came up behind me, snatched the pencil out of my hand, and made some fast dark lines on my paper.

"Like that," he said.

I didn't understand what he meant. Then I sort of did. I was having trouble getting the whole figure on the page. My nude was sort of cut off above the knees, and my gorilla had a head too big for his body.

"Change," Arnold Zweiback said.

The model grabbed a stool and kneeled on it with her arms around the gorilla's neck. I flipped to a new page. This time I did slightly better, only the model looked like maybe a little bird sitting on the shoulder of King Kong.

"Change."

This time she sank to the floor and lay at the gorilla's feet. I knew I didn't have a chance of getting this one right, so I just drew the woman, and the gorilla from the knees down. At the end of five minutes I actually had something better than I expected. What I had drawn might be a human. The gorilla legs were a failure, though.

After the break, we had a thirty-minute pose. I got everything on the paper, using my eraser a lot, and Arnold Zwieback came and made marks on my drawing twice. He also spoke to me.

"You seem to have a feeling for the gorilla."

"Well, I've always liked them," I said.

It was the hardest work I had ever done. Actually,

I think it was the only work I had ever done. I was per-spiring. I was concentrating. I also felt sort of embar-rassed that my drawings were so stupid. I think I felt way more naked than the model. I got some comfort from glimpsing what the others were doing—most of their stuff stank too. I noticed the others made a point of not looking directly at anybody else's drawing.

I understood now why they all looked depressed coming in.

Except this one guy. Blond guy. He was hand-some, like Ralph Noble. He was drawing with a pen! He drew standing up, with his arm extended, and it looked like he was conducting an orchestra. He drew the girl and the gorilla with these smooth, curving thick and thin lines, and he could do three beautiful drawings on one sheet of paper without any mistakes in five minutes. I wanted to be him.

"Okay! That's all, folks," Arnold Zwieback said. "We're here every day. Come back whenever you want. Meanwhile, draw from nature, draw still lifes, draw from imagination. Rome was not built in a day. Don't get discouraged. Bye-bye."

CHAPTER 12

Ugly Mug

The drawing students began flipping their sketchbooks shut and putting their pencils and charcoal and erasers and rags in their various boxes and bags. Most of them moved fast so nobody could see their drawings. The few who didn't, except for the blond maestro, didn't have anything a great deal better than what I had done. Of course, their stuff was better—actually lots better—but not worlds and universes better. There didn't seem to be any reason why I could not develop the level of skill they had within a reasonable amount of time.

I calculated that the fifty I had from Emil Pfiff, keeping back maybe ten dollars for some art materials, would buy around a dozen classes. If I neglected to mention to my father that I had swapped music for art, the three-fifty a week would continue, so further supplies and lessons would be covered, along with the odd hot dog. And maybe Billy Zwieback would arrange a freebie once in a while if I helped him carry stuff or clean up. I craned my neck to see his drawing board. As the son of the teacher, I figured he ought to be pretty advanced. What Billy had drawn was a series of little square panels, like a comic book, and in the panels he had drawn the gorilla chasing the model, and the model chasing the gorilla—nothing to do with the poses. The style was familiar, sort of like the newspaper strip *Beetle Bailey*.

"*De gustibus non est disputandum.*" It was the chick from the Art Institute. She was looking at Billy's cartoons too.

"What is that, French?"

"Yes. It means, 'Everybody has their own taste,'" she said. "So, did you look at the painting?"

We were outside on the corner by this time. The two muffled maniacs were still buzzing around the spooky white house, slapping on the whitewash.

"It did things to my brain," I said.

"You're not the only one, bud," the chick said. "By the way, my name is Jenny Thimble."

"I'm Harold Knishke."

"Oh, like the song!"

"The song?"

"Yes, 'The Ballad of Harold Knishke.' Blind Beet sings it," Jenny Thimble said.

"Blind Beet?"

"He's a folk singer. You never heard of him?"

"Never. And he does a song called 'The Ballad of Harold Knishke'?"

"It's pretty good. He sings fairly often at the Ugly Mug—that's a coffee house where it so happens I am a waitress. You ought to come some night. You can hear a song all about you."

"I might do that. Where is it?"

"It's on North Park, just north of North Avenue, on the west side of the street."

"North Park, north of North, on the west side," I said.

"You can't miss it. The first cup of coffee is on me."

"Thanks."

"After that, they're a dollar apiece."

"Pretty steep."

"Well, there's entertainment."

"I get it."

"Okay, well, I should be going."

"Right."

"I'll see you here at class, I suppose."

"Sure."

"Or at the Ugly Mug."

"Right."

"Okay."

"Bushman lives."

"Right."

And she was gone. This conversation had gone on a lot longer than the one on the Art Institute steps. I thought I had handled myself pretty well.

CHAPTER 13

I Am Surprised

It turned out that the dime store had quite a decent art supplies section. I bought a variety of pencils, charcoal, and erasers, a package of crayons, a bottle of India ink, and some drawing pens. I also bought three sketchbooks: large, medium, and pocket-size.

I found I could fit everything except the two larger sketchbooks in my empty flute case, after I pried out and threw away the velvet-covered insert with spaces for the taken-apart flute.

When I got back to the apartment I found my father home from work early. He had a job with the Chicago Salami Council down at the Sausage Mart, a big building near the Loop. It was because of his job that I had to get hot dogs on the sly and away from home. We never had sausage of any kind. "Once you've seen it made . . ." my father often said.

"Don't tell me!" I would say.

"Time enough for you to learn," my father would say. "One day, after you graduate, you may need a job, and I can use my connections to get you something in a sausage factory. Then you'll know. Meanwhile, why shouldn't you enjoy your childhood and be spared horrible dreams?"

"I have no desire to work in the sausage industry," I would tell my father.

"Who does?" he would say. "But it can be a steppingstone to an excellent career. Look at me—I work in an air-conditioned office, associate with fine people, and only have to come in contact with actual salami once a year at our annual banquet, and even then nobody expects me to eat any."

This time, there was no mention of ground-preserved meats. Instead he said, "What have you got there, sketchbooks?"

"Um . . . yeah." I wasn't prepared with an answer.

"You going in for drawing?" my father asked.

"Well, I thought I might," I said. "Just to see if I can, you know."

"Did I ever mention that I went to art school?" he asked.

I was surprised. "You did?"

"Sure. Two years I went . . . nights. While I was working in the banger department at Shlup Brothers. But then I got married, and you came along, and the job at the council opened up, and I sort of let it go. It's a great thing, drawing. You don't have to be talented. You can draw at the level you're at. Now, those flute lessons I pay for every week—I don't know. I never hear you practicing, but I have a feeling you stink. If you're not musical, what's the point?"

I wondered if Emil Pfiff had called him and ratted me out. "So you wouldn't care if I didn't keep on with the flute?"

"What kind of an instrument is that, anyway?" my father asked. "I mean, it's never going to get you girls. You don't show up at a party and everybody asks you if you brought your flute. So, show me some drawings."

I had my drawings from Arnold Zwieback's life class folded up in my back pocket, along with the coverless book Christmas Royal had given me. I was a little hesitant to show my father, what with the subject being nude, but I actually wanted an opinion. I dragged them out. "They're not very good," I said.

My father looked. "Oh, you've been to a life class. See, you're not getting the whole figure on the page. She sort of runs off the edge of the paper at the knees, and in this one she only has half a head. Same thing with the gorilla. Did they actually have a gorilla there?"

"A stuffed one," I said.

"Well, it's a matter of practice," my father said. "You need to go a couple times a week, and keep at it. What did it cost you, this life class?"

"I got in for free this time," I said. "I sort of know the son of the guy who runs it. But it's three-fifty per class."

"I tell you what," my father said. "Give up the nonsense with the music lessons and I'll cover the cost of the drawing class. I'd rather you didn't hang out with musicians anyway. They take drugs and skip out on their rent. And if you want, you can sell the stinking flute and keep whatever you get for it."

I was about 90 percent sure Pfiff had called him, but I didn't want to complicate what was already a fairly confusing conversation. "That's just what I'll do," I said.

"Fine," my father said. "When you get better you can draw my portrait."

CHAPTER 14

A Little Night Reading

Modern Art, An Invention of the Devil?

BY REV. NATHAN DUNORD, B.A., M.A., F. R. ECON. S.

Archimandrite of the First Reformed
and Apostolic Jewish Church of Memphis Tennessee

INTRODUCTION

The reader will no doubt be aware that the Impressionists were nothing but a bunch of un-washed, wine-swilling Frenchmen who sat around in cafés or pursued dirty women at the end of the nine-teenth century. Of course Van Gogh was a Dutchman, which is worse. And Toulouse-Lautrec was a tiny little fellow who drank like a fish.

The activities of these parasites and degenerates gave rise to Cubism, Fauvism, Futurism, Pointillism, Constructivism, Orphism, Surrealism, Dada, and also Impossibleism, Supersurrealism, Dynamic Double-Dog Realism, Ishkabibbleism, and Mama, which is like Dada only nicer.

All of these movements were taken seriously for some reason, and are generally supposed to constitute the early history of modern art. In this book, I propose to show that the work of this assemblage of mentally deranged individuals is unimportant and should not be considered the real story of the progress of Art. To do so, I will first present the history of art, from the beginning of time, in a few pararaphs.

Cave Painting. This was good. Primitive humans painted animals on the walls and ceilings of caves, and why shouldn't they? After a long day of chasing mastodons, your caveman stayed up late painting one. If we still had people like that, this would be a better world.

Egyptian Art. Also good. They were religious folk, and painted gods and things. They also built pyramids, and made gigantic sculptures for everybody to enjoy.

Greek Art. The Greeks were good sculptors at first—later they changed from making statues of people standing up straight with staring expressions and their fists clenched and went in for cute people, which was a mistake. Their paintings and mosaics— not so good.

Roman Art. The Romans copied the Greeks. Also lousy painters, and so-so sculptors. I am not dealing with architecture in this book—but theirs, and the Greeks', was okay if you like columns.

Medieval Art. In the Middle Ages, they got everything right. Inspired by constant warfare and the Black Plague, the artists of that time did wonderful things. It also helped that nobody could read.

Renaissance Art. Things got even better. Oil painting was invented, also perspective, and trade flourished so there was plenty of money to spend on art. Different countries and regions developed different styles, and individual artists became famous. Everybody had a lot of fun.

At this point, I started to get a little bored with Reverend DuNord's list and started skipping ahead, reading a page or two here and there. I wanted to get to the modern art part and see what he had to say about that.

What he had to say was that all art was pointless or fake, except art depicting birds, especially ducks.

According to him, the greatest artists of all time were a guy named John James Audubon and whoever painted the covers of the L.L.Bean catalog. He also thought that Donald Duck was great art, which I agree with up to a point. But what was clear was that DuNord was a raving lunatic and nutbar. But that did not mean it was not a useful book. I had long since learned at Riverview High School that bad and insane teachers can still teach you things—including not to trust what anyone tells you.

So, on a page in my medium-size sketchbook, I copied all the names of the artists he mentioned, almost none of whom I had ever heard, and also the names of the different art movements and periods in the history of art.

CHAPTER 15

In the Rwenzoris

Sun comes up. We feel warmth. Night was cold. Pull big leaves around. Sleep close to others. Now light. Green stuff is wet. Lick. Stretch. Taste this one. This one is good. Soft. Chew. Wants to play? Chase him. Chase me. Ha ha ha ha. Run. Fall over. Falls on me. Ha ha ha ha. Eat this leaf. This one is good. Now everybody eats leaves. Quiet. Chew. Sun warm.

Everybody moving. Go up the mountain. Find good green stuff. Smell green stuff. Taste. This female is mother. Carried me then. Now touches me. Eat this leaf. Breathe.

Everyone lies down. Green stuff smells good. Feet in air. Lie in green stuff. Big male is watching.

Nothing to fear. Smell. Breathe. Feel sun. Lie flat in green stuff. Mountain is good. We fall asleep.

Bang bang bang! Young male makes noise. Little ones run to females. Bang chest. Show teeth. Scared. Ha ha ha ha. Not scared. Bang bang bang bang. Scream. Run. Shake green stuff. Ha ha ha ha. Fall down. Eat leaf. Sun is good.

This one is friend. We go. Find good green stuff. Eat eat eat eat. Friend next to friend. Eat. Mmmm.

Wait! Where is everybody? Moving again. Up mountain more. Climbing. Little ones running. They make noise. Ha ha ha ha. This is good. Fog. Air is wet. Good smells. Other green stuff. Eat. Good. Now sun. Now fog. Air is good. Other ones, males, females, little ones, good. Mountain good. Green stuff good. Big trees. Good good.

CHAPTER 16

Harp Music

Professor Seymour Waldteufel, dominant force in the Anthropology Department at Lake Forest College, is enjoying high tea in the Palm Court of the Drake Hotel, where he resides. Clad in a rich pinstripe, Waldteufel is of impressive size, with immense shoulders, powerful arms, beetle brows, and piercing brown eyes.

There is harp music, the delicate clinking of fine china, and the murmur of polite conversation in the elegant room. Waldteufel, a vegetarian, is addressing a large fruit salad. With him at his table is Nancy Watanabe, one of his students.

"So, here is an article from *Life* magazine, June 26, 1950. 'Bushman is Sick' is the title, and the first paragraph tells about the time Bushman fell ill in his cage," Waldteufel says.

"The next paragraph gives some statistics—six foot two, five hundred pounds, twenty-two years old . . . and worth a hundred thousand dollars, having cost thirty-five hundred when he was acquired by the zoo as a baby.

"Then the article gives his history. 'An orphan baby gorilla,' it says. This causes the reader to think the zoo did him a favor by taking him in. It does not mention that he was an orphan because his mother was shot to death before his eyes. The claim is made that he was suckled for a year by a 'native woman.' That suggests some kind of special bond between the ape and humans. I'd like to see the native woman robust enough to breastfeed a two-year-old gorilla, which is what the article states as his age at the time of capture.

"It goes on to say that his keeper dare not enter his cage because of his great strength, even though he is not as mean as Gargantua, the Barnum gorilla. 'Not as mean as.' You see, Bushman is nice, affable, the recipient of kindness from humans, and at the same time dangerous.

"Then the article tells how Bushman was revived

with digitalis, but at twenty-two was nearing the end of his life—twenty-two for a gorilla being equivalent to seventy years old for a human. In fact, twenty-two years for a gorilla is more like thirty-four years for a human.

"And Bushman did die, later that same year. The cause of death was publicly given as heart disease. The fact that he had a severe dietary deficiency, because the zoo did not know what to feed him, was not published until years later.

"And here is another article, from the newspaper, with the heading 'Bushman Finally Gets Gas Chamber.' Bushman's stuffed and taxidermied skin is displayed at the Field Museum in a glass case filled with poison gas to prevent moths and insects. But the heading plays on the idea of Bushman, a convict behind bars, going to the gas chamber as if for execution.

"Oh, and going back to the *Life* magazine article, directly following it is another article, headed 'A New Batch of Gorillas.' This tells of a brand-new shipment of baby gorillas brought in by Trefflich's, the animal dealer in New York. Trefflich is quoted about Arno, one of the new gorillas, 'He is beautiful. What an animal! He bit me in the calf. He hates people already!'

"Now, Miss Watanabe. I think you might review some of this material, do a bit of research, and come

up with some conclusions about what the captive gorilla means in our society, whether there is some kind
of relationship to certain widely held prejudices and
folk beliefs, and . . . Miss Watanabe, why aren't you
eating your French pastries? Miss Watanabe, are you
crying?"

[Redacted]

The author has determined that this chapter is unsuitable for a general readership.

On the Bus

On the bus, carrying him to the Great Lakes Naval Training Center, Geets Hildebrand had a pleasant conversation with a young woman who appeared to be of Asian descent. She told him about the article she had been reading in a scholarly journal.

"It's about the Belyaev experiment. It seems this Russian geneticist, Dimitri Belyaev, was sent to Siberia to find a way to help with the fox farming industry there. The workers complained that the foxes were vicious and hard to handle. Belyaev had the idea that by selecting the least vicious foxes and mating them with other foxes that showed the least fear and aggression, the result would be a strain of docile animals, easier to handle.

"It worked out exactly as Belyaev expected. In a very few generations, they were getting foxes with less fear of humans, and less tendency to bite. What Belyaev was not expecting was that other behaviors changed too—the foxes began to bark like dogs, whine like dogs, come when called by name, and wag their tails like dogs.

"Even more unexpected were physical changes. The specially bred docile foxes began to show broader skulls, floppy ears, wavy and curly fur, and colors and patterns that wild foxes do not have . . . black and white patches, speckles and spots, piebald white blazes on their foreheads."

"In other words, they turned into domestic dogs?" Geets asked.

"More or less," the young woman said.

"What does the experiment mean?"

"Well, for one thing, it proves the theory of evolution, which some people still doubt, largely because it isn't mentioned in the Bible, and more interestingly, it shows that instead of happening over hundreds and hundreds of years, evolution can happen fast—*snap!* In no time at all.

"Oh, here's where I get off," the young woman said.

"Bushman lives," Geets said.

"Bushman lives," she said.

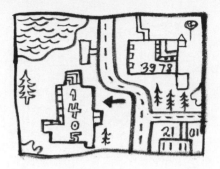

Non Sibi Sed Patriae

A little while later, Geets got off the bus at the Great Lakes Naval Training Center, midway between Chicago, Illinois, and Milwaukee, Wisconsin, and showed his pass to the guard at the gate, who handed him a small map showing directions to Building 1405.

The Ballad of Harold Knishke

I got to be fairly addicted to drawing. I went to the life class a couple of times a week. After a while, Arnold Zwieback had Billy Zwieback and me drag the gorilla back to the shop he had borrowed it from and bring back some African shields and spears, which were easier to carry and fun to play with. Again, I got a free class for helping.

What I had learned so far was that drawing is about seeing, and the thing the life class does is lock you into looking at the model—and there's another pair of eyes, in this case Zwieback's, checking and making sure that what you put on the paper is what is actually there to be seen. Some of the more advanced drawers develop style, but the point is to train the eye. It's not as much about the hand. I got to understand that drawing like that is like playing scales if you're learning to play music—something I never understood or did when I was doing that.

Unlike scales, it was not boring. In fact, it was fascinating. There were different models, male and female, all different shapes and sizes, and every one of them presented different problems for drawing. Also, just seeing a variety of people naked was interesting. They just came in and posed. There wasn't any conversation except sometimes a few words during breaks. The drawers were busy concentrating, and the models were busy posing. So you didn't get to know the models, and I found myself trying to figure out who they were, what sort of people, just from how they looked. Sometimes after class when the model came out of the dressing room with clothes on, it was like a different person—you wouldn't recognize them on the street even though you had just spent two hours looking at them. People have different faces with their clothes on.

Besides drawing in class, I drew constantly everywhere I went. I drew everything. I couldn't stop drawing. Like I said, I was addicted. This was because I had begun to see things differently. It was a little like what happened when I came out of the Art Institute after looking at the painting by de Kooning, only that time it was involuntary, and confusing—there wasn't any understanding in it. It was like suddenly a big orchestra was playing and I was just listening. Now I was starting to see how things were put together, how some lines were pleasing, how light changed things, how shadows worked. Now everything was interesting to look at. I could sit at a table in some lunchroom and the napkin holder, knives and forks, a half-eaten hamburger, a glass, could be complicated and beautiful.

I didn't get to know the other people in the drawing class very well. I knew Billy, of course, and had a nodding acquaintance with some of the others, but they were all older than me, and smoked. Sometimes Jenny Thimble was there, and she always talked to me. I also would exchange a few words with her when I went to the Ugly Mug to drink expensive coffee and draw the beatniks.

CHAPTER 21

Ol' Haro Knshkkgg

I had been to the Ugly Mug on North Park north of
North a few times, but Blind Beet had not been there
on the nights I attended, so I had not heard the song
Jenny Thimble always mentioned to me. I couldn't
go very often because the dollar per cup for coffee
made a hole in my funds, and would have bought me
a sketchbook. Jenny slipped me a freebie a couple
of times, but obviously she couldn't always do that.
One time there was a Dutch folk singer there—he was
all right, but I was glad it was one of the times I got
free coffee. Another time there was this tall, amazing, beautiful black woman with a voice that made
my brain vibrate. If she had been there every night, I
would have gone broke coming to listen to her.

It was a cool place. The tables were gigantic spools that had been used to wrap cables around. You sat on crates. On the spool tables were candles in wine bottles with wax drippings all over them. Jenny and the other waitresses were all dressed in black, with pale makeup. And the patrons were interesting. There were a lot of beards. Also sandals. The standard costume for women was a black leotard on top and a skirt made out of a Indian bedspread. There was plenty to draw, even though the place was pretty dark.

Finally I hit the place on a night when Blind Beet was there. He was up on the little platform with the microphone when I came in, just beginning his set. He had a beat-up twelve-string guitar and was wearing an old-fashioned double-breasted suit and a baseball cap. He was around ninety, and had no teeth and a Delta accent as thick as grits. I couldn't understand a word he said. When he got around to "The Ballad of Harold Knishke," the beatniks started applauding when he played the first few chords of the intro.

The song went like this:

    Ol' Haro Knshkkgg he wah wah mmmmm
        hmmm goo.
    One day Haro he blng ga frooo.

Haro Haro wha chezgonga dooo?
Ol' Haro Knshkkgg wah wah wah
Ol' Haro Knshkkgg hoobahdoo

. . . and so on.

Whang whang whang, went the guitar.

When he finished the song, Jenny Thimble snatched up a flashlight and pointed it at me. "Ladies and gentlemen, I give you the real-life Harold Knishke!" she shouted.

The beatniks applauded. "Ol' Haro Knshkkgg! Ol' Haro Knshkkgg!" they shouted.

I got up and took a bow. It seemed like the only thing to do.

And I got a free cup of coffee.

CHAPTER 22

Artistic District

I developed a routine. I would leave the house early in the morning with my flute case full of drawing materials, a cheese sandwich, and a sketchpad.

Usually I would start out drawing trees and the lakeshore in the park and work my way down to the zoo. Drawing the zoo animals was something I enjoyed. Hoofed animals were the best because they stood still a lot. I did good drawings of the greater kudu, the lesser kudu, zebras, and gnus. The gnus were sort of challenging, because they don't make sense in the way they look—I mean, they aren't exactly rational in the way they're designed, so you have to look hard and not assume anything about the way they're put together. I learned from trying to draw them that I had a tendency to put on the paper what I thought I should be seeing rather than what was actually before me. And I made the connection with things that were wrong with my drawings and other people's drawings in the life class. They'd be looking at the model but drawing an image that was in their head, not what they were actually seeing with their eyes. The gnus, also called wildebeest, taught me about that, and it was good gnus.

I always looked in on the gorillas—they were admirable specimens, and I liked them, but of course not one came anywhere close to being Bushman.

I also learned stuff reading the cards attached to the animals' enclosures—for example, the horn of the kudu, which is wavy and pretty, is used to make an African musical instrument called the kuduzela, and also the shofar, which is a horn used in Jewish ritual.

From the zoo I would make my way to North Avenue, which is one of the main streets in Old Town, the artistic district. This was where the beatniks assembled, and I was getting pretty comfortable with them, and trying to fit in. I had sandals my father gave me— he got them on a trip to Florida and never wore them again. I tried growing a beard, but gave it up after a week because it was growing in patches and looked disgusting. So I bought a pipe off the card behind the counter in the Nor-Well Drug Company, and a package of tobacco, London Dock—which smelled, I suppose, like London docks. The pipe was a giant Rhodesian, it cost $1.49, and looked similar to a pipe Vincent Van Gogh is smoking in one of his self-portraits. I decided, rightly I think, that carrying the musical instrument case and the sketchbook, plus the pipe, was enough to make me look authentic.

Old Town did not have any actual sidewalk cafés like they have in Paris, where Van Gogh and Toulouse-Lautrec and those guys used to sit and sketch and argue about art. I wanted to have an argument about art with someone, but I didn't know anyone likely to have opinions I could argue with—nor did I have any opinions yet. I would have settled for overhearing an argument about art, but without the sidewalk cafés, it didn't seem likely. There were a few folding chairs and a couple of tables on the sidewalk outside the Nor-Well Drug Company on the corner of North and Wells. You could get a cup of coffee at the counter inside and take it out and drink it while sitting in the street. It wasn't a cafe, but it was the best thing available. I would get coffee and eat my cheese sandwich there, and try to do fast sketches of the other street-sitters and people passing by.

I got to have a nodding acquaintance with other

Nor-Well regulars, and sometimes got into conversations with them. This gave me a chance to practice beatnik speech, which all of them spoke. It is fairly easy—you say "man" a lot and try to sound like Marlon Brando, and that's all there is to it. Also, to sound like a beatnik you express surprise in an unsurprised tone about unsurprising things. Here is an example of an actual conversation in beatnik speech in which I myself participated while sitting outside the Nor-Well Drug Company:

"Man . . . that's a green car. Dig."

"Yeah. Man. Green."

"Green."

"I dig it, man."

"Yeah."

The pauses are important, and the word "dig" can be used anywhere. You can address both men and women as "man."

CHAPTER 23

Street People

Probably the most interesting person I got to know, sitting outside the Nor-Well Drug Company, was Eddie Balchowsky—he had lost a hand fighting in the Spanish Civil War, which I had never heard anything about. It seems that in the 1930s a bunch of Spanish generals who wanted fascism rebelled against the elected government and got a lot of help from Nazi Germany and some big American corporations that supplied them with trucks and tires and stuff. Some Americans helped as individuals, mostly by going and helping the Republic fight the fascist rebels. Eddie was one of those, and he lost his hand. The Republic lost the war, and a little while later other fascists in Germany started World War Two. We got into that war against Germany, so General Motors, and Ford, and Firestone tires couldn't help them. Eddie was a poet and painter and musician—he played piano one-handed—and sometimes sang songs in Spanish from the civil war.

A close second to Eddie Balchowsky for being interesting was Anderson Punch, also known as Casey Jones, and mostly known as the Chicken Man. This is the guy that apparently every citizen of Chicago has seen some time or other, going around with a trained performing chicken. The chicken would dance on command, play dead, collect dimes and bring them to her master, drink beer from a bottle cap, and ride around on the Chicken Man's head, nestled under his hat. For unintelligible speech, next to Casey Jones, Blind Beet was Sir John Gielgud—again, no teeth, and a down south accent dating from the year 1870—but Balchowsky appeared to understand him, and they would have a little chat while I furiously tried to draw them.

Other regular sidewalk sitters included Jerry the Junkie, who was pleasant and funny, but sort of stuck to the subject of his drug habit, of which he appeared to be proud. He said he was the only public relations man for narcotics. There was a guy whose one and only interest was a concoction made of protein powder, blackstrap molasses, wheat germ, bonemeal, honey, and figs, which he drank by the quart, and which, he claimed, would give the user spectacular health. He demonstrated this by whipping off his hat and showing how the health drink was curing his baldness. He had five, maybe six, hairs on top of his head—but, he claimed, those were new, and before long he would have a whole crop.

There was also the Indian yogi, who always wore a nice suit, and showed me some breathing exercises— I'm not sure what they were supposed to do for me. There was a guy with a bushy beard who was a philosopher, the guy with the army cap who had used me as a demonstration at Bughouse Square, a few people I knew from the life class, and an assortment of people, some of them normal, who would stop by for a coffee and some conversation. Everybody talked to everybody, and everybody said "man" a lot. It was like a club. I had never belonged to a club. I spent about an hour there every day, sketching, exchanging a few words with the others, and sucking on my giant Rhodesian.

CHAPTER 24

How I Was Doing

Billy Zwieback turned up at my sidewalk club one day. I bought him a coffee. I was craving an opinion about my progress with drawing, and for some reason I didn't feel like asking his father. Even though Billy drew nothing but comic strip cartoons, I figured he'd been around art his whole life and might know something. So I asked him.

"Don't ask me," he said. "I don't know anything about art. Don't ask my father, either—all he's interested in is teaching drawing."

"What? Doesn't he do paintings and stuff?"

"He used to, but he was no good at it. He's good at drawing figures, and that's all he cares about. It's like this—if you were an athlete, let's say you were a shortstop for the Cubs, you might work out in a gym, besides actually playing baseball. There would be other people working out in the gym too; some of them couldn't catch a baseball or get a hit to save their lives, but they would be doing the same exercises, and maybe even doing them better than you, the professional baseball player. It wouldn't have very much to do with what made you able to play."

"So, what are you saying? This stuff I'm doing isn't art?"

"It might be. I have no way of knowing. To me, it's drawing, and I would say you are doing really well, considering you just started. I'd say some of your stuff approaches being mediocre."

"Really?'

"Sure. You can be proud."

"While we're on the subject, why do you do cartoons instead of drawing the model?"

"I don't know. I think I have brain damage."

"Interesting."

CHAPTER 25

Art Mystery

So, I found out the first lousy thing about being an artist. You can't tell if you're making progress or if what you're doing is any good. You can tell if you like something you're doing, or if it feels satisfying after you've done it, but you can't tell if anyone else will react the same way—and you can't trust people to be honest and tell you if they actually like something, because they may try to be polite, or they're confused and don't know their own taste, or think they aren't qualified to express an opinion about art. But other peoples' opinions is not the lousiest part of it—it's the fact that the artist himself is never sure.

For all I know, Rembrandt would say to himself, "This painting is turning out to be garbage, but I guess I'd better finish it so I can get paid," and all the time he would be working on some monster masterpiece and not know it. And some of the artists around Old Town were extremely proud of stuff that a cat could have painted. In fact, there was one case known of a cat having better taste than a human.

It was this guy named Clark Gomez—he was a big hulking idiot, and a painter. Everybody agreed that he was the worst painter in the world. His stuff was not just bad, it was painful to look at. He was a good-natured fellow, and had lots of friends—of course, nobody ever told him his paintings were a disaster. He had a job in the produce department of a supermarket, and he would bring home peppers and carrots and paint them. Only the paintings didn't look like peppers and carrots, or paintings. Maybe they looked like nightmares peppers and carrots would have if they could dream. And had no imagination.

One day a cat walked through his window. It was a big shaggy cat, and Clark Gomez decided to keep it. He got dented cans of cat food for free at his job, and the cat decided to stay with him. He named it King Kong. When Clark worked on paintings, King Kong would watch him attentively. He would look at him and the painting with a fixed stare. Clark said he could feel the cat's eyes burning a hole in him. He said the cat made him nervous. When the painting was finished, Clark would lean it against the wall and have a look at it. The cat looked too. Then King Kong would react in one of two ways. Some paintings he would go behind, then curl up and go to sleep. Clark would slap white paint on these and use the canvas for another painting. Other paintings King Kong would attack and try to claw to death. These paintings Clark Gomez would put in a high rack attached to the ceiling where the cat could not reach them. He would crate up the paintings King Kong hated and ship them off to juried competitions all over the country. Every one of them won first prize, some of them were bought by museums and collectors, and articles were written about Clark Gomez in magazines—not mentioning the cat.

One day King Kong went out the window he had come in by, and never returned. Clark's paintings went back to being lousy. He got another cat, but it wasn't interested in art. He continued to paint, and was promoted to assistant manager of the produce section at the market.

CHAPTER 26

So Here I Was

So here I was—I had been an artist for three whole weeks, and all of a sudden I didn't know if I had any talent. I remembered my years of flute lessons—of course, in that instance I had sort of known all along that I couldn't play.

I remembered what my father said, "You don't have to be talented. You can draw at the level you're at." I thought about it. I actually went to see Clark Gomez in his studio. He let me in and showed me his paintings, which made me feel slightly sick. He gave me a ginger beer, just to be friendly—but it helped with the nausea. He said if I ever needed any advice or painting lessons, to just drop in again. He had four or five cats and a girlfriend. He seemed a perfectly happy person.

When I left Clark Gomez's studio, I was still confused, but I wasn't worried.

CHAPTER 27

It's a Great Lake
if You Don't Weaken

"Senior Chief Horowitz? Recruit Gustave Hildebrand, reporting as ordered."

"Come in, Hildebrand. Your nickname is Geets, isn't it?'

"Yes, Senior Chief."

"Sit down, Geets. Let's have a talk."

"Thank you, Senior Chief."

"How are you getting along with your training, Geets? Do you like the navy so far?"

"Senior Chief, I like it very much, and I am enjoying the training."

"You're not homesick, are you? Have you ever been far away from home before?"

"Senior Chief, I am not homesick, and I come from Chicago, which is no more than an hour away."

"Getting along with the other recruits? Are any of the instructors giving you a hard time?"

"Senior Chief, my shipmates are swell, and so are the instructors."

"So you are completely happy in boot camp? That's very unusual. We try to make it difficult on purpose, you know."

"I am completely happy, Senior Chief. I never got to go away to summer camp, and I always wanted to. I have learned to swim, tie knots, fight fire aboard ship, and all kinds of neat things as a navy recruit. And I love the food."

"So why have you been contemplating suicide, Geets? Answer me that."

"I have not contemplated suicide, Senior Chief, and may I say I am enjoying this clever psychological interview. If you have ink blots for me to look at, I am ready."

"Geets, have you or have you not on several occasions climbed to the top of some of the larger buildings on this base, and did you or did you not do so with the idea of flinging yourself off and plunging to your death, only each time you lost your nerve and did not do it?"

"Senior Chief, I have climbed to the top of *all* the larger buildings on this base, and I wish to state that I did so on my own time, during on-base liberty, and was wearing approved navy-issue attire for athletic activities. I did so with the idea of climbing back down and not of flinging and plunging. Also I was careful not to harm the buildings in any way."

"Why did you climb the buildings, Geets? Why?"

"Because they are there, Senior Chief."

"Geets, you understand that as a sailor in the United States Navy, you are required to follow orders, and that is mainly what we train people to do here at the Recruit Training Center. If I were to order you to quit climbing buildings, would I be correct in assuming you would obey?"

"Would these be navy buildings, or all buildings of every kind, Senior Chief?"

"All buildings of every description, for the entire time of your enlistment."

"Naturally, I would obey, Senior Chief. But I would take exception to the order on the grounds that as a sailor in the United States Navy, I consider it my obligation to maintain physical fitness, and climbing is excellent exercise. Also, I would ask if obeying such an order would preclude my climbing a building if a commissioned officer or petty officer subsequently ordered me to in the course of duty, for example to rescue the president of the United States, who had somehow gotten trapped high up on a building, whether belonging to the navy or some other building."

"That is not very likely to happen, Recruit Hildebrand."

"Senior Chief, we are taught in our classes here at the Recruit Training Center that a sailor should be prepared for the unexpected. I don't mean to suggest that I know better than the navy, but I would think that instead of ordering me to stop climbing buildings, it would be more useful if you had me teach other recruits how to do it."

"Geets, I have reviewed your record. You are a good recruit. The navy likes you. But we think it might be better if you were to go back and finish high school. It would not be a less than honorable discharge. We have something called an entry-level separation. You could reenlist at a later time, possibly when you don't feel as much of a need to climb buildings. Or maybe you would like to consider another branch of the service. I believe the army has a mountain division—all they do is climb things."

"Of course, if the Senior Chief thinks that would be best."

"I do, Geets. You are a fine, if weird, young man, and it has been a pleasure to meet you."

"Senior Chief, one thing more . . ."

"Yes?"

"Am I permitted to keep my dungarees, high-top basketball shoes, and denim shirt?"

"Yes. Also your navy-issue underwear, socks, and canvas sea bag, and you will be paid for the time you have served."

"Thank you, Senior Chief Horowitz. That is more than fair."

CHAPTER 28

Zion

A tall youth entered the general store of John Fergusen, in Zion, Illinois, not far from the Wisconsin border, and close to Illinois Beach State Park. Something about the youth's manner and appearance alarmed Fergusen at first—he suspected shoplifting or possibly a holdup, and considered telephoning the police. But the young man simply wanted to purchase some canned goods, candles, matches, clothesline, a small tarpaulin, and an aluminum cooking pot. All this he put in a canvas duffel bag.

"Going camping?" Fergusen asked.

"Yes. It's something I've always wanted to do."

"Well, have a good time."

"Thank you, shopkeeper," the young man said.

Known primarily for the beach, Illinois Beach State Park includes dunes, wetlands, prairie, and woodlands.

More than 650 species of plants have been recorded in the dunes area alone, including dozens of types of colorful wildflowers. Prickly pear cactus thrives in large colonies in the dry areas, and the wet prairies are carpeted with a wide variety of grasses and sedges. Large expanses of marsh in the swales support dense stands of cattail, bluejoint grass, prairie cordgrass, reed grass, and big bluestem.

The sandy ridges are crowned by black oak forests with an open, savanna-like appearance and several kinds of fragrant pines.

Just north of these pines is the Dead River, which actually is a stream that is blocked by sandbars much of the year, forming an elongated pond. When the water finally rises high enough, it breaks through the sandbar and drains the surrounding marshes. The abundance of aquatic plants and fish flourishing in this changing environment provide a vivid contrast to its name.

Camping is limited to designated areas, and nude bathing, nude romping and flower-gathering, and nude cookouts are discouraged, but since much of the park is inaccessible to police cars and it falls between the jurisdictions of the town of Winthrop Harbor and the unincorporated village of Zion, the rules are generally unenforced.

Despite its proximity to the cities of Kenosha, Wisconsin, Waukegan, Illinois, and Chicago, the park is relatively underutilized and has a deserted wilderness aspect at times. Fauna includes a rich variety of birds, deer, raccoons, skunk, squirrels, opossums, and muskrat, all of which are native to the area and might be expected, but local residents claim to have glimpsed bears of unusual shape and size from time to time, which naturalists consider highly unlikely and most probably unsubstantiated rumor.

CHAPTER 29

On the Rocks

There are these big rocks that line the lakeshore. Everybody calls them "the rocks," but they are really quarried stone, big cubes of it several feet on a side. They're arranged like a set of gigantic steps leading down to the lake. On the park side you have to haul yourself up to get on top, and in a couple of places there are crude steps made of piled-up stones, a kind of miniature of the big ones. Once you are on top, you're looking down a few steep levels to the surface of Lake Michigan. It's really kind of neat. In a thousand years or two, archaeologists will speculate about the rocks as though it were Stonehenge and wonder what strange rites primitive Chicagoans performed here.

Well, some of the strange rites are not to be mentioned in polite company. The "steps" are plenty wide enough to spread a blanket, and on hot summer nights, lots of people go there to sleep. They treat the rocks as they would their bedrooms. I will say no more except if you go there at night, show good manners walking along, which would include staying on the top level to avoid stepping on the backsides of people at their most vulnerable. In the daytime, it is mostly fishing. There's not much swimming off the rocks, except maybe at high tide, because once you're in the water, getting out and up to the first step is sort of impossible, and you'd have to swim a long way parallel to the shore all the way to the end of the rocks at Oak Street beach, and then, assuming you hadn't gotten exhausted and drowned, it would be a long walk back to where you left your clothes.

I was sitting on the rocks, trying to draw the lake—I mean draw the water. This was difficult. I wasn't able to get anything on paper that anybody could possibly think was water. I was coming to the conclusion that maybe it was impossible to draw water with a pencil—maybe I needed some kind of paint, watercolors. I was pretty intent on trying to draw, and had not noticed this girl sitting not far away with a huge dog.

At first I thought it was a child, because she was child-size, but she had breasts, and hands and feet of an older person about my age, large hands and feet. The dog had big feet too.

"You see anything out there?" the girl asked me. She was peering out into the lake, shading her eyes with her hand.

"Lake," I said. "Water. Some clouds."

"That's all?"

"Sure. What else should I see?"

"You don't see anything like an island, by any chance?" she asked.

"Nope. And as far as I know, there aren't any islands around here."

"Well, none that are easy to see," the small girl said. "But there is supposed to be one that is mostly invisible. I just thought maybe you being an artist and all, you might have the ability."

"I'm not an artist," I said. "I'm just trying to draw."

"Okay. Sorry I interrupted."

"No, that's okay. I'm not getting anywhere anyway. That's a nice dog, by the way."

"He isn't a dog."

"What is he, a wolf?"

"Not a wolf either. He's the Wolluf."

"Okay."

There was a silence.

"What's a Wolluf?" I asked.

"The Wolluf. He's what you call *sui generis*. There isn't another one—just him. He didn't always look like this, like a dog. It just amuses him to do so. I brought him with me from New York."

"You come from New York City?"

"Not the city. From the mountains. My name is Molly—what's yours?"

"Harold Knishke."

"Oh, like in the song. Listen, if you like drawing, maybe you should meet Victor. He's all about drawing and painting and stuff like that."

"Victor?"

"This guy. We're staying with him at the moment. He's the one who sent me out to look for the island. He's batty on the subject of the island. He's been trying to find out if it's really there for like thirty years."

"What is he, like an adult?"

"Like."

"So what's the Wolluf's name?"

"I told you. He's the Wolluf. Doesn't have a name to my knowledge, other than that."

All this time, the Wolluf was peering out over the lake.

"Let's go," Molly said.

"Go?"

"Yes. I'll take you over to Victor's place and introduce you. You might find it interesting."

"Okay."

"Okay, let's go."

CHAPTER 30

Walking and Talking

So I walked along with Molly, and the Wolluf, her wolfy dog who was supposedly not a dog and not a wolf. Molly told me her last name was DeDwerg and she came from this Dutch New York family that went back hundreds of years. She said she left the Catskill Mountains because her people were too old-fashioned, and then she got involved with this friend of hers— as near as I could make out, the friend was schizophrenic, or had a dual personality or something like that. Anyway, the friend either thought she was two people, or there were two people who thought they were one person, and Molly said it got so complicated, she felt she needed a break, so the Wolluf suggested they both go to Chicago for a while.

"The Wolluf suggested?"

"Yes. Well, he's been here before."

"And you wound up with this Victor. Who's he, and how did you come to know him?"

"Friend of the Chicken Man," Molly said.

"The Chicken Man? The old guy with the chicken who rides around on buses talking gibberish?"

"Him. He's like Victor's oldest friend."

"And you knew the Chicken Man how?"

"The Wolluf knows him."

"The Wolluf knows him."

"They were in Hollywood together in the silent movie days. The Wolluf was an actor, played mostly dogs."

"Figures."

"Well, he played a famous one called Rin Tin Tin. He was like the biggest movie star there was for a while. Oh, I forgot to mention—back in New York, before we came here, I was crazy for a while."

She'd read my mind.

"But I got cured by this old wise woman. I'm studying to be one too. And I didn't even know this at the time, but she—get this for an astounding coincidence—is the Chicken Man's great-aunt."

"She must be like a hundred and seventy-five years old."

"She is. Anyway, here we are."

CHAPTER 31

Here?

We were in front of the white house, the one across the street from Zwieback's drawing class! "Here? This is where you're taking me?"

"Sure. It's Victor's place."

"We're going inside?"

"Why not? It's interesting on the inside."

"'Why not?'! This is a spooky place. Something strange goes on here!"

"Stranger than you could possibly guess—but, like I said, interesting."

"This is the place where two muffled-up types are constantly whitewashing the outside!"

"They have to do that."

"They do? Why do they? Why do they have to do that? It's weird and insane!"

"Save the questions. If you think the outside is weird, prepare to be rocked and shocked when we go in."

"I don't know," I said.

"Don't be a weenie," Molly said. "You'll like it. Come on, we go around the back."

If a small, big-handed, big-footed girl could go inside, I could. But, I was a little scared as I followed Molly and the Wolluf down a narrow passage beside the house. There was a little concrete backyard, and a little back door, completely covered with whitewash, of course. Molly turned the whitewashed doorknob, and we went inside.

Inside. Inside the place was huge! I mean, it was huge! It was gigantic! It was impossibly larger than the house appeared on the outside. It was like an airplane hangar, maybe as big as a football field. But that was not the most incredible thing—incredible was the walls and ceiling. It was all one big space . . . and they were . . . they didn't seem to be made of wood or anything solid. It was like being on the inside of a balloon, and like a balloon, it was all translucent, and mostly transparent. You could see everything outside the house in a slightly fuzzy way. I felt dizzy.

"Fairly neat, is it not?" Molly asked.

I think I said something like "Duh." Here and there the floor of the huge open space was divided into little areas. Some were irregular cubicles, open at the top, and made of plywood and two-by-fours. Others were open spaces with furniture arranged as though it were a room, and others just had objects, like cigar boxes or assorted items of trash marking where walls might be—and some just had chalk outlines drawn on the floor. In some of the spaces were people, doing things—I was too stunned and mixed up to focus on anything, or what the people were doing.

Molly snapped me out of it. "Now do you get why they have to keep whitewashing the outside?" she asked me.

"Because there isn't any house," I said. "There is just the whitewash, which obviously isn't whitewash as it is generally known, but some substance nobody ever heard of." I could see the form of one of the bundled-up characters through the roof, against the sky, brushing the stuff on. "And they have to keep applying it or the place would evaporate or collapse or something."

"I knew you were smart!" Molly said. "Now, let's go meet Victor."

CHAPTER 32

Victor

Victor was probably around forty, but he looked younger. He was bald on top, and had a wispy beard. His cubicle was a regular office cubicle, walls made of plywood or something, painted a sort of office gray-green, and the top parts of the walls made of sheets of opaque glass. He was sitting in a swivel chair, with his feet on a beat-up steel desk.

"Oh, it isn't mine, and I didn't invent it. I don't really understand how it works—they just let me use it."

"Who?"

"The ones whose invention it is. It's an experiment. The stuff we keep slopping on the house only lasts about forty-eight hours, max. If that can be licked, it could be the basis for a whole new kind of architecture. The outside is solid. You can kick it, or drive a nail into it—just as though it were a regular, real house. As you can well imagine, there isn't anything like this anywhere else."

"Yes, I can well imagine. I can hardly imagine what I am seeing right now," I said. "I mean, the outside is sort of miraculous, but the inside is just crummy cubicles knocked together out of scrapwood and stuff."

"Well, that part is my idea," Victor said. "Since there's this space, and I'm the manager, or the caretaker, or whatever you care to call me—actually I'm just sort of here in case anybody comes along, the city or someone, and wants to know whose property this is, or who lives at this address—I thought it would be a good idea to use the space for something, so I thought this up."

"And this is?" I asked.

"It's a workshop. Better to say a bunch of little workshops, or offices, or studios. Mostly it's artists who need workspace, but there are people working on all kinds of projects. There's a mathematician who's calculating the precise thickness of strings to make the best-sounding guitar, and a comedian-zoologist who is rehearsing a routine performed completely in the vocalizations of howler monkeys. I'm told the act is a scream. There's a guy who's considering becoming a philosopher—he sits in his space and thinks. But mostly it's artists."

"Harold is an artist," Molly said. "He draws."

"Well, okay, Harold," Victor said. "Let's say you want a place to work on your drawings, keep your materials and finished pictures—you can come here, and if you agree to the rules and I think you'd fit in all right, you can make a space to work in . . . you can drag in hunks of wood you find in alleys or wherever and build a cubicle, or just mark out your space on the floor with chalk, whatever you like. Then you can do your drawings, and you can leave things here. Nobody will bother your stuff."

"Do you charge rent?"

"Nope. It is free."

"What are the rules?"

"Basically, everyone has to agree not to talk about this place, and the unusual nature of the outer shell, and not bring people in here who might talk about it. You understand, because it is a secret experiment, the architectural part."

"Molly brought me in here," I said.

"But Harold is an artist and would like to make a place to work in," Molly said. "And you promise not to tell people about us, don't you, Harold?"

"Sure," I said.

"Well, there you are," Victor said. "Molly did right."

"So, what are you saying? I can come in here and claim a space to work in?"

"Do you want to?"

"Yes, I sort of do," I said.

"Fine. Move in anytime. We're open around the clock. Oh, and it goes without saying that you may not show anyone pictures of the interior of this place, or what goes on here."

"Got it," I said.

CHAPTER 33

Black Panthers

"Do you do some kind of work here yourself?" I asked Victor.

"Mostly I work on scrapbooks," Victor said. "Here. You can look at this one."

He handed me a big floppy scrapbook. On the cover he had printed *Black Panther Sightings*. I flipped through the pages. It was a collection of clippings, mostly from newspapers. Each told about the sighting of a very large black cat in some unlikely place, such as a Little League field at night, or a backyard in the suburbs, or a shopping center. Victor had drawn a circle in green crayon around articles in which the person reporting the sighting was someone in a position of trust—a chief of police, a doctor, a teacher, a priest. There were hundreds of clippings, and they appeared to go back for years.

"This is interesting," I said.

"You see the point, don't you?" Victor asked me.

"Sort of," I said. "It's that there are black panthers of some kind all over the United States?"

"It proves a theory," Victor said. "I assume these cats are pumas, also called mountain lions. They're native to the continent, and a long time ago they were everywhere. As the population grew, they were hunted to extinction . . . most people believe. But what may have happened is that the shier, more reclusive, and cleverer mountain lions escaped being hunted. They became more and more nocturnal, because it was easier to avoid humans that way, and the darker cats had an advantage because they were less visible in the dark. So, generation after generation, dark and elusive cats mated with other dark and elusive cats and produced dark and elusive offspring, and ultimately evolved into a race of black pumas that are seldom seen. Now and then someone gets a glimpse of one, as the clippings show."

"Evolution," I said. "I heard that some people don't believe in evolution. They say it's just a theory, and it's more likely that God just created everything like it says in the Bible."

"I have an answer for that," Victor said. "If we were created by God, just as we are, we'd have been designed better. Why would God create a human with lower back pain, like I get from time to time? But if I evolved from an animal that went on all fours, it would make sense that my body might not be that well suited to standing upright."

"Sounds reasonable," I said.

"Oh, evolution is going on all the time," Victor said.

CHAPTER 34

Wise Woman

"I assume you have a space here," I said to Molly. "What is it you do?"

"Come along, and I'll show you," Molly said.

Molly took me all the way to the limit of the enormous space, where the end zone would be. On the way, I noticed that some people had created workspaces in clusters, and others were off by themselves. Hers was way off by itself. She had made a sort of screen or topless tent out of old sheets and bedspreads propped up with mop handles and poles of wood.

"Here's my little area," she said. There were a lot of orange crates, stood on end to make cabinets, full of jars and bottles, and little paper bags, a reading lamp and an electric hot plate with an iron pot on it. Something was simmering in the pot—it smelled like applesauce. I noticed that the hot plate was not plugged in. The plug was lying on the floor, but the thing was obviously hot. The same was true of the lamp plug lying on the floor. I switched it on. It lit up.

"That's sort of unusual," I said.

"One of the properties of this place," Molly said. "And don't ask me how it works."

I noticed a rolled-up sleeping bag. The Wolluf was using it as a pillow and drooling on it. "Do you sleep here too?" I asked her.

"Sometimes. Us Dwergs don't sleep a lot. It's a trait."

"Insomniac."

"Dwerg."

"So what exactly do you do here?"

"I told you. Studying to be a wise woman. It's herbs and potions, poultices, remedies, cures for schizophrenia—things like that."

"What's that cooking in the pot? It smells like applesauce."

"It's applesauce."

"For curing?"

"For eating. I practically live on the stuff."

"You can cure schizophrenia?"

"Sure. You have a problem?"

"No, just curious."

"Well, that one is fairly advanced. I can't actually do it yet, but potentially."

"But you consider it to be possible."

"It worked for me."

"Cool."

"The Wolluf wants to wander around the town," Molly said. "Any questions before we go?"

"Um. Does this place have plumbing?"

"Theres a water spigot and an outhouse in the backyard."

"Seems kind of primitive, considering the magic electricals."

"Hey, it's rent-free. And it beats where I come from. Anyway, you live in a nice apartment. I may come by to use your shower sometime."

"My parents will be delighted to meet you. How do you know I live in a nice apartment?"

"It's in the song: 'Old Harold Knishke, he lived in a nice apartment.'"

"Oh, right. The song."

"Well, we're on our way. I'll see you around, no doubt."

"No doubt. Thanks for bringing me here."

CHAPTER 35

Lizardlips

On my way out I observed a couple of things. One was that evidently Billy Zwieback was a fellow tenant. His space was marked off by a rope that was attached to a bunch of toilet plungers stood on end, so I was able to see the stuff he had assembled. He had a drawing table, and a stool and a lamp. I knew it was his space because I recognized his drawing style—the cartoons. Pinned to the drawing table was what he was working on—it was a comic strip. The title was "Ol' Harold Knishke." The drawings showed a character who looked nothing like me but smoked a pipe and had a sketchbook under his arm and a pencil behind his ear. As far as I could tell, there was no story and he wasn't doing anything.

The other thing I observed was the two ragamuffins who did all the whitewashing. They were taking a break: eating bologna sandwiches on white bread and smoking mentholated cigarettes. In order to eat and smoke, they had pulled their face scarves down just enough to get at their mouths. Under their floppy white work gloves, I could see they had very skinny fingers, and their lips were thin, like lizard lips.

CHAPTER 36

Turning Nocturnal

Summer in Chicago gets to be so hot, you go crazy. Sometimes you feel like the temperature is trying to mug you, to beat you up and leave you for dead on the pavement. Around the Fourth of July is the last time anyone can breathe normally. People with air conditioners stay inside a lot, and people without air conditioners, which is most people, are driven out into the street. This is when everybody becomes an insomniac. They stay away from their houses and apartments until the rooms have cooled off a little. Some people just drag blankets into the park and sleep there, or on the rocks along the lakefront. Others set up card tables and chairs and play pinochle or dominoes, or read under streetlights until the small hours of the morning, or sit on steps in front of buildings, or go to all-night movies, which are air conditioned.

People talk freely to strangers. Since everybody is exhausted, and half undressed, people feel informal and strike up conversations. Most citizens of Chicago know a fair number of people they've never seen in a good light. Mostly I sort of like the hot summer nights, and feel sorry for people who have air conditioners and miss all the social fun—other times I wish we had one.

We could have one. We live in a nice apartment, and my father certainly makes enough at the Salami Council to be able to afford one—but it is out of the question. My mother has an unreasonable fear of them. She believes the air that air conditioners puff out is tainted in some way, and apt to bring on disease. Not only is there no talking her out of this, but she is one of those people who is always cold. She will wear a sweater on days when other people are clinging to the ground like reptiles.

My father belongs to a bridge club, which is an apartment he and a bunch of other bridge nuts rent. He spends most nights there, more so in summer. The place is air conditioned to a ridiculous degree—like a skating rink. There is a strict rule not to bother my father there except in case of genuine emergency, which has never come up, or if he calls home to have something brought to him, like his reading glasses, or a hundred dollars in cash. This has happened a couple of times, so I have seen and experienced the place, which is furnished like a regular apartment but with lots of tables and chairs, and people playing bridge with jackets and sweaters on—never mind it is ninety-nine degrees Farenheit and humid outside. In the bridge club it is no more than fifty.

This summer, I had my own cool place to go— cool in more ways than one. The communal studio in the incomprehensible white house was always a pleasant medium temperature, and the air was fresh, which was also incomprehensible—along with the fact that electric appliances worked without being plugged in—since there were no windows or any recognizable method of ventilation. I had set up my own little studio with an old floor lamp I found piled by the curb along with an orange crate, a folding chair, and a rickety folding table. All this stuff I dragged to the house. I had chosen an area off by itself, not very far from Molly's space, and claimed it by drawing an outline on the floor with a piece of chalk.

Not many people used the house late at night. In fact, it was mostly deserted. The lizard-lipped whitewashers might be napping in a large crate of wood shavings—apparently the miraculous coating on the outside only degenerated in sunlight, so they got some time off. Once in a while, Victor would be in his cubicle, working on scrapbooks. And there was this guy, there every night, listening to records he played on an old-fashioned floor-model Victrola fitted with a pair of clunky-looking war-surplus headphones.

Although my space was supposed to be a studio, I wasn't able to do any drawing. There was nothing to draw. There was nothing in the place but space, and it was so vast that the items of junk people had dragged in were dwarfed by the bigness and amounted to nothing. Plus, it was dark, except for the few puddles of light from the un-plugged-in but lit lamps. Imagine a deserted football stadium on a dark night, with just the few little glowing spots. I tried drawing the place with ink and a brush and wound up with pieces of paper sort of completely covered with black. So I would make tea on Molly's hot plate, with permission—she was never there—and read Tarzan novels by the light of my floor lamp until I was cool enough and bored enough to go home, or just stretched out and slept on the floor.

CHAPTER 37

Wake Up! This Is Important!

Someone was shaking me. And someone else was licking my face. It was Molly, and the Wolluf was licking me. His breath was fairly horrible. I had gone to sleep on the floor, using a copy of *Tarzan and the Forbidden City* as a pillow.

"What? What's important?"

"Go out back and wash your face," Molly said. "Then come with me. There's someone you have to meet."

"What time is it?"

"I dunno, two in the morning? Come on, wake up."

"What do you do, wander around all night? Don't you ever sleep?"

"Not much. Come on, get yourself organized. We have to go."

The thing about Molly is it would never occur to anyone not to do whatever she tells one—or offer to prevent her from doing anything she wants to do. She stood by as I splashed water on my face.

"Okay. Let's go. You have your sketchbook? Good."

"What's this about?" I asked her.

"I found you a mentor."

"A mentor?"

"Yes. Someone to guide you and tell you what to do."

"I need that? How do you know?"

"I know. I told you, I'm studying to be a wise woman. You need this guy. Now hurry up—we want to get there before he leaves."

Molly was skittering along the sidewalk. The Wolluf was loping. I had to half run to keep up with them. "Where are you taking me?"

"Bignose's. He's always there around this time."

"Bignose's Cafeteria?"

"Yes. They're open all night."

"They won't let you take the Wolluf inside, you know."

"Why not?"

"Because Board of Health rules, or the law or something. You can't take dogs into restaurants."

"He's not a dog."

"Oh, right. I forgot. He's the Wolluf."

"Less talking, more walking."

"Can I ask you why you think I need this mentor or whoever it is?"

"No."

CHAPTER 38

Bignose's

Golyat Thornapple was scruffy and his clothes were rumpled. He needed a shave, and his white hair looked as though he had cut it himself with dull scissors. His shoes were cracked and scuffed, and he had no socks. He was sitting at a table near the window, eating a broiled porgy. He saw us.

"Good golly, Miss Molly!" Golyat Thornapple said. "And a young friend, and here's my good old boy." He scratched the Wolluf behind the ears. Molly was right about him being allowed into the cafeteria. Nobody said a word.

"Mr. Thornapple, this is Harold Knishke," Molly said.

Golyat Thornapple smiled warmly and stuck out

his hand. He seemed to be a nice old guy. "Harold Knishke, like the song," he said.

I shook his hand. "Bushman lives," I said.

"He certainly does," Golyat Thornapple said.

"Harold wants to be an artist," Molly said. Thornapple's expression changed. For a second I thought there was a fish bone stuck in his throat. "I was hoping you could give him some advice, maybe look at his work. Tell him what to do."

"This is a vile trick to play on a man while he's eating," Golyat Thornapple said.

"I'm going to get you a Napoleon, and a nice cup of coffee," Molly said. "I'll get one for you too, Harold. You sit here and talk with Mr. Thornapple. Why don't you show him your sketches?" Molly hurried off to the counter to get us Napoleons, whatever they were.

I stood beside the table, under which the Wolluf had gone to sleep. "This was not my idea," I said. "She just dragged me here."

Thornapple was eyeing my sketchbook. "You may as well sit down," he said. "Molly's a Dwerg, you know."

"So she has told me."

"Best not to refuse when she asks you to do a thing."

"Is that so?"

"Oh, yes." Thornapple pushed his plate of porgy bones aside. "Let's have a look." He leafed through my sketchbook, making occasional noises like "Hmm" and "Mmm" and "Aha." Then he handed it back to me.

Molly returned with a tray with three Napoleons, which turned out to be these yummy pastries, and three cups of coffee, also a raw hamburger Bignose had given her for the Wolluf. We sat and munched and sipped for a while.

"Did you get around to the advice?" Molly asked.

"Here it is," Golyat Thornapple said. "Don't be an artist."

"No?"

"If possible, don't."

"Why not?"

"Many reasons, but for one, if you become an artist there's a good chance you will wind up as a crazy old bum eating porgies in a cafeteria in the middle of the night."

"That actually sounds sort of okay to me."

"Too bad. What makes you think you want to do art in the first place?"

"To tell the truth, I'm not absolutely sure I do want to do art. It was just something I said, and then I stumbled across Arnold Zwieback's life drawing class.

The idea occurred to me, kind of out of the blue, after I'd been listening to this guy in an army hat speaking at Bughouse Square."

"Sergeant Gunter. I know him well."

"He was explaining how capitalism is bad—and I could see he had a point, but at the same time, I got the feeling that socialism or communism, or whatever he's selling, is probably just as bad, and the problem is human beings can ruin anything, even if it's a good idea to begin with."

"Well, at least you've got a brain, Harold. So how did you get from being skeptical about political enthusiasts to thinking you should be an artist?"

"Maybe I should be an artist."

"Maybe."

"I would say definitely, not maybe," Molly said.

"Answer the question," Golyat Thornapple said.

"Well, it's not that I have a lot of experience outside of being a kid and going to high school, but . . . um . . . but if human beings are hopeless idiots, which appears likely . . . maybe art does the least harm."

"Interesting idea," Golyat Thornapple said.

"Harold is smart," Molly said.

"Also, I want to be cool," I said.

"Like me," Golyat Thornapple said.

"Right."

"You definitely have the hopeless idiot thing right. Let me ask you three questions."

"Okay."

"Not counting the time you marched through with your fifth grade class, how many times have you been inside the Art Institute?"

"Um . . . approximately . . . once."

"Once."

"Well, I'm planning to go back."

"Good. See, you can't do art if you have never looked at any art."

"You can't?"

"Well, you can, but then you have to invent the entire history of art all by yourself, which would take a while. No need to go nuts and try to eat up the whole collection—but I suggest you drop in every day or so and look at a picture, by which I mean *look* at it . . . with your eyes."

"I can do that. What are the other two questions?"

"Can you swim, and do you get seasick?"

"Yes, and I don't think so. What do those have to do with learning to be an artist?"

"Nothing. I was just curious."

CHAPTER 39

See You Around

"**W**hat did you think of Harold's sketches?" Molly asked Golyat Thornapple.

"They're sketches. He's learning to draw. Cavemen could draw."

"And Harold can come to you for advice, and you'll look at his stuff, and help him?"

"Do I have a choice?"

"Of course you have a choice. Nobody's forcing you. If you don't want to help Harold, you don't have to."

"But then I would be refusing a favor to a Dwerg," Golyat Thornapple said.

"True."

"And that could be an unlucky thing to do."

"Well, superstitious people might believe that."

"Harold may come to me for advice."

"Of course, granting a favor to a Dwerg *is* a lucky thing to do, and that's a fact."

"I don't feel I have been coerced or threatened at all, and thanks for the Napoleon and coffee."

"My pleasure, Mr. Thornapple."

CHAPTER 40

What's a Dwerg?

We were walking away from Bignose's. It must have been around four in the morning.

"Mr. Thornapple seems sort of cynical and depressed," I said.

"He's just moody. He'll be happy soon, when something nice happens to him."

"Something nice? Like what?"

"I wouldn't be surprised if the Art Institute bought one of his paintings . . . or something like that."

"Explain this Dwerg thing to me," I said.

"DeDwerg. It's a family name. We're well known."

"What are you, like the Mafia?"

"Nah. The Mafia are criminals."

CHAPTER 41

Painting with Troika

The first picture I picked out to look at with my eyes at the Art Institute was by this guy Wassily Kandinsky. It said on the card he was French, born in Russia in 1869, and died in 1944. The picture is called *Painting with Troika,* and he did it on January 18, 1911.

The reason I picked this to look at was that I liked it. I liked it right away, the first second I saw it. They had a few others by him, and I liked them, too, but this is the one I picked to look at. I looked at it for a pretty long time, maybe twenty minutes, and all the time I was feeling that it was in some way friendly and familiar. Here are a few things I noticed about the painting—the colors were bright and clear, it was sort of simple in a way, like a kid's kindergarten painting.

This made me feel happy. Also like a kid's painting, he didn't try to show things arranged with the earth or floor at the bottom like a straight line, and the objects in the painting piled up on top as though they were solid and had weight. I forgot to say, it is an abstract painting, and the thing that is supposed to be a troika, which I looked up, and it is a kind of wagon or carriage pulled by three horses, could be a troika, or maybe not—it's kind of up to you. Behind the troika there is this blue thing with what might be roofs on top, then to the right is a flowering tree, or a bunch of flowers, then this thing that is pretty certainly a hill, and in front of that what might be a couple of people, one of which is holding some kind of musical instrument—maybe. It's all maybe. Oh yes, and there were mountains, or maybe ocean waves, at the bottom. Kandinsky didn't try to draw anything so it absolutely looked like some real thing. Also things did not appear to be solid, or stationary. It was as though everything was in motion, maybe spinning slowly.

And then I realized why I liked it, and why it seemed familiar. My father has these bound copies of *Krazy Kat,* which is a newspaper comic strip from the 1920s, done by this guy named Harriman. Krazy Kat and Ignatz the Mouse are the main characters, and mostly they hit each other in the head with bricks. And yet it is funny, and I have always liked looking at it, because the drawings, while very simple, are also very interesting. And they look almost like if Kandinsky wanted to draw a comic strip, it might look something like *Krazy Kat*. They were alive at the same time, so maybe Herriman had seen paintings by Kandinsky. Or, for all I knew, Kandinsky had seen *Krazy Kat*. Or maybe each of them had seen something else that gave them the idea to draw like that. Or maybe some optician had given them both the same kind of wrong glasses—I can't say. But it was interesting to think about. And the Kandinsky picture made me think of music. *Krazy Kat* would be like someone whistling a tune, and the painting would be like someone playing maybe an accordian or a harmonica. It made me feel good—full of energy. I could have done a little dance in front of the picture.

When I came out of the Art Institute, I had a similar experience to the time I had looked at the de Kooning. Not as extreme or surprising, but things had a fresh look. I was going to have to look up my mentor, Golyat Thornapple, and ask him if this was supposed to happen every time.

CHAPTER 42

I Buy Some Colors

I went to an actual art supplies store in the Loop. It was pretty fantastic. They had about a million art supplies. The guy in the store suggested I try these colors called gouache. They come in tubes like oil paint, but they're water-based. He said they weren't as demanding technically as oils or watercolors, and you can get some neat effects if you mix them with diet cola or cold coffee instead of water. I got the beginner's set, and some brushes. Everything fit in my flute case.

CHAPTER 43

Street. People.

Geets Hildebrand had made a nice little shelter using his tarpaulin and clothesline, in a stand of trees, concealed by a little sand dune. He had made a nice little bed using pine boughs and the blanket he had stolen from the United States Navy. He had gathered stones and made a nice little fireplace, on which he heated cans of corn, okra, string beans, and cream of mushroom soup for his meals.

He spent his time picking up wood to burn in the fireplace, improving his campsite, observing the birds, and exploring the park. There did not appear to be any other campers, and in fact he did not see another person. He discovered a street that ran along the boundary of the park, on the other side of which was a little neighborhood of well-kept houses. So he had a good idea of where the kids he found standing in his campsite one morning when he crawled out of his shelter had come from.

There were three of them, two boys and a girl, all quite substanial and robust-looking.

"What are you doing?" one of the boys asked him pleasantly.

"Camping," Geets said.

"How long have you been here?"

"Couple of days."

"How long do you figure on staying?"

"I don't know. Until my food runs out, I guess."

"Is that what you've been eating?" the girl asked, pointing to the little pile of empty cans.

"Sure."

"Would you like to come back with us and have pancakes?"

Even before they offered him pancakes, Geets had felt there was something unusually kind and sweet about these kids. They looked at him with a calm and steady gaze, and their eyes were full of love. They seemed completely relaxed and comfortable. In the few minutes he'd been talking to them, Geets realized that most people have a little edge of aggression, or readiness to defend themselves or flee, always bubbling somewhere beneath the surface. These kids didn't have it. It could have been because being tremendously strong, as they obviously were, they had nothing to fear—but it seemed to Geets that they had within them a molten core of goodness that radiated like warmth, which he had never encountered before . . . except in himself. That, too, was a realization that came to him in minutes—that he had that same inner glowing something, and his was communicating with theirs.

"Did you come out before breakfast to find me?" Geets asked them, not knowing why he did.

"Well, Mom wondered if you'd like pancakes."

They knew he was there. Probably knew the minute he arrived. Geets was not surprised.

"I would perfectly love pancakes," Geets said.

"Well, let's go then!"

And they trooped off through the woods, Geets and the three big kids, whose names he did not even know, all of them already the best of friends.

CHAPTER 44

At Home with the Hugebees

Charles, Nancy, and Russell were the kids' names. They were the children of Sterling and Monica Hugebee, who were also large and strong-looking. Mr. and Mrs. Hugebee, like their children, projected that same quality of sweetness, and Geets fell instantly in love with them, too.

The house had lots of windows, and many easy chairs, sofas, large, soft cushions, and thick rugs. There was a deck behind the house, with padded porch furniture, recliners, two hammocks, and a large table set with plates, carafes of coffee, and bottles of maple syrup.

"Sit down, Geets. Sit down, everybody," Mrs.

Hugebee said. "Pancakes start coming in five minutes!"

Blueberry pancakes, pancakes with raisins and bananas, chocolate chip pancakes. They were the most delicious pancakes he had ever tasted, as Geets knew they would be. The family talked pleasantly while they ate stacks and stacks. They asked Geets questions— he told them of his recent enlistment and separation from the navy. They told him about their little neighborhood right beside the state park, and about their neighbors, a couple of whom dropped by—the Lobelias. The Lobelias were cat groomers. They had a cat-grooming salon attached to their house. The Hugebees were spoon benders.

"Spoons come from the forge perfectly straight," Mr. Hugebee explained. "But a fine spoon has to have a subtle curve to it, and this can be done only by a skilled craftsman. We are the ones who do this."

Other neighbors were the Bananamans, accountants who kept the books for the other family businesses in the neighborhood, and the Fernblatts, who made marzipan chipmunks and other animals. The children of the families were all homeschooled, and since the street the houses were on was a dead end, except for deliveries of supplies and pickups of manufactured items and groomed cats, few vehicles, and hardly any people, ever came to the neighborhood.

"We like living in a quiet place," Nancy Hugebee said.

The pancake eating, which had been going on steadily, came to an end, the conversation faltered and halted, and the Hugebees, the Lobelias, and Geets sank onto the chaise longues, and into the hammocks, and slept in the morning sunshine.

CHAPTER 45

Geets's Dreams

Geets Hildebrand sometimes vaguely remembered a dream, or a category of dream, different from his usual dreams. This dream was unusually vivid and seemed real in every detail. When he woke he would be convinced it was real—it seemed every bit as real as his waking life—and yet he would always forget it after a few minutes. In this dream, or dreams, he was always in another place, always the same place, and there were characters and events that carried over from dream to dream. Time continued from dream to dream, and the events of the past remained the same. It was no different from days in his real life, waking up in Chicago, and being who he was and having seen and done what he had seen and done. If these dreams did not fade completely after five minutes, and leave his consciousness, he might have entertained the thought that possibly the dream world was the real world, and his day-to-day life in Chicago was the dream life.

The setting of the dreams was a quiet, usually sunny, place. There was a feeling of well-being and safety. He was surrounded by gentle people. He was content and happy.

Napping on the deck of the Hugebees' house, full of pancakes, and breathing regularly, Geets dreamed his dream, and when he awoke, the place he was in was no different from the place he had dreamed.

Everyone else woke up at the same time, stretched, nodded to one another, and as a group, the Hugebees, the Lobelias, Geets, and some people from the other families in the neighborhood crossed the road and entered the park.

There, they rambled through the woods and over the sand dunes, along the lakeshore. They observed the bird life, identified various plants, threw pebbles into Lake Michigan, waded barefoot, commented on the beauty of the clouds and sky, and several times sat down, all at once, and had a mini-nap. Loretta Fernblatt, a girl Geets's age and twice his size, walked beside him, and sometimes held his hand. He was perfectly happy.

Sterling Hugebee asked Geets if he could swim and if he was ever seasick.

Geets reminded Mr. Hugebee that until very recently he had been a recruit in the navy, so the answers to those questions were yes and no, and why did he ask.

"Just curious," Mr. Hugebee said.

That evening, practically the whole neighborhood gathered on the Hugebees' deck, and Mr. Hugebee, having set up a screen and projector, ran silent Laurel and Hardy movies.

CHAPTER 46

You've Heard of Adolf Hitler, I Suppose

Golyat Thornapple had a studio not far from the corners of Diversey, Clark, and Broadway. It was at the top of the Diego Forlan Apartments. Everybody in the building except Thornapple was from Montevideo, and the landlady was a former zonal beauty queen. I had taken to visiting him there to get advice about art and life.

Thornapple's studio was cluttered and messy. He had a lot of paintings he had done, some pretty good ones of gorillas, and also lizards in ballet shoes and tutus. I wasn't sure if I liked them. I also wasn't sure if Thornapple liked me. It may have been that he only tolerated me because he did not want to incur the displeasure of the DeDwergs—but he seemed reasonably happy, or at least not unhappy, to see me, and talked to me, which was something.

"So, I suppose you're a Zen Buddhist," Golyat Thornapple said.

"I beg your pardon?"

"I thought all the young people were Zen Buddhists nowadays. In my time we were communists."

"I don't even know what a Zen Buddhist is."

"It doesn't matter."

I had visited Golyat Thornapple three or four times before I noticed that the stuffed owl on his mantelpiece was not stuffed but actually a live owl.

"He came with the apartment," Thornapple said. "Was here when I moved in. He catches a mouse now and then, and the landlady brings him the occasional torta frita. An owl can be good company."

"Mr. Thornapple, I recently became aware that the Art Institute, besides running a museum, a gift shop, and a cafeteria, also has a school of art. Do you think it might be a good idea if I were to enroll?"

"Well, it might—but art schools can be tricky. You've heard of Adolf Hitler, I suppose."

I said I had.

"Were you aware that it was Hitler's youthful ambition to be a painter? He applied to the Vienna Academy of Fine Art in 1907, and they decided he wasn't talented enough to be in their school, and turned him down. So he went on to become a dictator and mass murderer and started World War Two. Now, I have seen a couple of his paintings—not very interesting, but who knows, he might have improved—and even if he hadn't, he would not have taken up much room in the art school, and if they had let him in, there's a chance he would not have later plunged the world into a vicious war and caused the deaths of millions of people and untold suffering."

"So, you're saying?"

"Art school can cause a lot of damage."

"Hmm."

CHAPTER 47

We Make a Deal

"Look," Golyat Thornapple said. "It wasn't my idea to be your guru, but you're a nice kid, and even though you've been warned, you seem to be fairly intent on learning about art. So, let's make a deal—I will teach you what you need to know, and you can assist me with various things. Does that sound reasonable?"

"It sounds fine," I said.

"But you have to agree to do what I tell you, follow orders as if you were in the army and I was your commanding officer. Would you be willing to agree to that?"

I nodded yes.

"Say it."

"I agree that if you will teach me about art, I will

assist you with various things, and I will follow orders as if I were in the army and you were my commanding officer." I saluted for good measure.

"Saluting is not necessary, and you will not have to call me sir. Here's a dollar and a quarter. Run down and get me a six-pack of beer."

"What kind of beer costs a dollar twenty-five for a six-pack?"

"Bullfrog Beer. They sell it in that place across the street. And I'm not going to share it with you, first because you're a minor, but also because it takes decades to get so you can tolerate the stuff."

"Is it a brand name or a variety of beer? Does it have any bullfrog in it?"

"One doesn't want to know. Get going. When you come back, I will commence educating you."

When I came back with the Bullfrog Beer, Thornapple handed me some kind of gourd with a metal pipe sticking out. There was hot liquid in the gourd.

"Here. Yerba mate, the tea of the gauchos. You sip through the silver straw. Get comfortable. We're going to listen to *Don Giovanni*." He had an old-fashioned record player, the kind that looks like a little suitcase. The lid was propped open, and there was a long-playing record on the turntable.

"What's *Don Giovanni*?"

"An opera."

"What? You want me to listen to an opera?"

"Not only listen." He tossed me a little booklet. "Here is the libretto in Italian and English, so you can follow the story."

"Why do you want to do this to me?"

"I'm educating you. We have a deal."

"About art. What does some opera have to do with it?"

"It happens to be the greatest opera ever written, or the second greatest after *The Magic Flute,* both of them by Mozart. There are differences of opinion. And we have a deal. Yours not to reason why."

"But opera is horrible."

"Orders is orders."

"What is it about, this opera?"

"It's about a jerk. He goes around seducing women, although he never actually scores in the whole opera. He has a servant he treats like dirt, and he kills someone, and in the end gets dragged off to hell."

"And this is the greatest opera ever written? Or second greatest?"

"Sip your mate, read along in the libretto, and when it's over you will tell me if you think it might be the greatest or second greatest opera ever written. Incidentally, this is a rare recording of the 1938 Glyndebourne Festival performance of the opera—this is your lucky day."

"How is this going to teach me how to be an artist?"

"Shut up."

More than three hours later, I had hardly moved. I am not sure I had ever sat still that long, or paid closer attention to anything.

"Golyat, this has to be the greatest opera ever written," I said. "It has to be the greatest anything ever written. How did he do that?"

"He was Mozart."

"The story is stupid."

"It's an opera."

"But it was the most exciting thing I ever heard."

"Right."

"Even though the story is stupid, and the people are idiots, especially that Don Ottavio, I was all involved in whatever they were singing about. He did it all with the music, right?"

"Right."

"And it was funny, then all of a sudden it was beautiful, and then it would get exciting, and when Leporello got scared, I felt pity for him, and when the

Don was being a complete schmuck, I sort of admired him for sticking to his schmuckness, and being brave about it. And then when the Commendatore dragged him down to hell, my pulse got fast and I was sort of scared myself. And at the end, after the Don was gone, I thought the people remaining were even bigger idiots than he was. And the whole thing is kind of cynical—like people are idiots, and the story makes fun of them . . . only when they express what they're feeling, it's beautiful and I kind of love them."

Golyat opened his fifth can of Bullfrog Beer. "Now you know something about art."

"But a painting couldn't do that, could it?"

"Could it?"

CHAPTER 48

On a Wall

"Well, I know that sometimes a painting can put your mind in a different place—I've experienced that already. It can be pretty powerful, and change the way you see things. But the opera had all these different musical ideas, one after another, and it took time to get through it all. I suppose if it was a really big painting . . . like on a wall."

"Okay, get out of here," Golyat Thornapple said. "I'm ready to go to bed. Drop around tomorrow after you've read up on murals."

CHAPTER 49

I Get the Idea

I struck lucky right away. The first book I found in the library was about a Mexican mural painter named Diego Rivera. His full name was Diego María de la Concepción Juan Nepomuceno Estanislao de la Rivera y Barrientos Acosta y Rodriguez. And he was big enough to carry a name like that. This was a wild guy—I mean, the things he did, and the places he went and the trouble he got into were beyond anything that could possibly have happened, but apparently they did. On top of this, he was married, on and off, to another painter named Frida Kahlo who was, if anything, wilder than he was. My intention was to just look at the pictures of murals he had painted, but

I started reading and had to check the book out and take it home to read the whole thing.

But already, when I was still looking at the book in the library, I was able to form an opinion about the murals. He put everything in them—historical figures, baskets of fruit, peasants, soldiers of the revolution, ancient pyramids, machines, skeletons, eagles, generals, famous people then alive, animals, gods. Little sections of the murals would have worked as paintings, but it was all one thing. Of course, these were just pictures in a book. I could only try to imagine them as huge, taking up whole big walls, and what it might be like to stand in front of one, taking it all in.

It wasn't Mozart—but I got the idea.

CHAPTER 50

Golyat's Story

Golyat Thornapple himself went to art school. This came out one night when I was sitting with him in his studio, drinking yerba mate out of a gourd.

"Did it do you any damage?" I asked him.

"Not directly," he said. "I had been off to war before I went to art school, so I knew something about taking care of myself. Of course, an art school was partially responsible for there being a war at all—so that has to be taken into account."

He left out that he did not simply go to war—he had to be dragged kicking and screaming. He said that it was not that he was afraid—just that seeming to agree with such a thing would suggest one hadn't given it any thought.

It would be clearer if I started at the beginning, having pieced together his life story from bits and pieces of things he said to me.

Golyat Thornapple had long hair as a youth, and often wore a cape. He was what he described as a fancy dancer, recited poetry on street corners, and sang Swedish folk songs, accompanying himself on an oud, which is an Arab lute. He consorted with the intelligensia of Chicago, drinking coffee with poets and philosophers in various bohemian bistros, and once had himself chained to one of the lions outside the Art Institute in protest that its modern art was not modern enough. His father, who worked in the meatpacking industry, and his mother, who was active in her church, did not know what to make of him.

When he received his draft notice, he ignored it. He also ignored repeated warnings from the authorities that if he did not appear at his local draft board he would be arrested. Then he received notice that he was going to be arrested. Finally, they came for him, and took him off in handcuffs.

He was taken to jail. Then he was taken, also in handcuffs, to see the draft board. "Are you a conscientious objector?" they asked him. "Do you have religious scruples that prevent your serving in the military? If you are a member of an organized religion that prohibits participating in war, there are ways we can accommodate you."

Golyat said he had no such religious principles.

"Are you a craven coward, or are you an agent of a foreign power, or an enemy of the United States?"

He said he was none of those things.

"Then why do you refuse to serve in your country's armed forces in time of war?"

Golyat explained that war is infantile, and nobody at all should agree to take part in one—and that he was just taking the reasonable position. He added that if everybody else were to do as he did and act on the promptings of his common sense, no war could be possible and a lot of trouble could be avoided.

So they threw him back into jail.

Every so often they would take him in handcuffs to see the draft board, where they would have the same conversation.

Then they would throw him back into jail.

This went on for months.

One day, possibly because he was tired of being in jail—he himself did not know why he did it—Golyat said he would agree to be drafted, and he signed something.

He was whisked away to the army. First was training—he was not treated nicely. The army suspected him of being a Nazi spy. "Are you a Nazi spy?" the officers would ask him. "Tell us who your Nazi spy friends are, and we will let you go back to Chicago." Golyat explained that he was not a Nazi spy, and had no Nazi spy friends. So they would make him crawl though the mud while live ammunition was fired over him.

Then training was over and Golyat Thornapple was sent overseas. He arrived in Europe and was just in time to be in the D-Day invasion. Then he got a telegram: "Come to London." It was signed by General Eisenhower.

In London, an officer talked to him. "We have been watching your progress since you were in jail in Chicago. You are a tough little fellow. You held out for a long time before agreeing to be drafted, and as you may have noticed, your training was extra unpleasant, and you held out against that. So, we think you would be perfect to do something secret for us. You would like to work on something secret, wouldn't you? We know you would. And if you tell anybody, you will be shot."

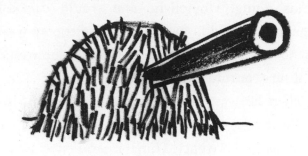

CHAPTER 51

Ghost Army

So Golyat went to work helping to camouflage things so they would look like other things when seen from the air—this was to confuse enemy bombers. Airfields would be disguised to appear to be farms. A haystack might conceal an anti aircraft gun, a barn could be an airplane hangar. A large factory for building aircraft or weapons might have a fake village built on its roof. Golyat liked this work, and he turned out to be good at it. He had many ideas, some of which were put into practice and others of which were rejected—such as his idea to disguise the soldiers as sheep. He found he liked working on a large scale. He got to design whole fake farms, and hoped to do a fake village.

Golyat wondered what was so secret about what he was doing. Obviously, one would camouflage things in war, and he was certain the enemy was doing it too. Why had the officer told him he would be shot if he ever told anyone what he did?

Then he was ordered to report to a unit in the actual war zone in Europe, the Ghost Army, officially known as the Twenty-Third Headquarters Special Troops. There were about a thousand men whose job it was to impersonate other U.S. Army units in order to fool the enemy. They used rubber inflatable tanks and guns, sound trucks with huge speakers over which they played sounds of trucks, tanks and marching soldiers, spoof radio transmissions, and such tricks as driving the same vehicles through villages again and again with different numbers painted on them, and having soldiers talk loudly in bars about battle plans so local spies and informers would hear and report bogus information. They were mostly quite successful. Golyat told me their biggest worry was that the Germans would someday bomb their rubber inflatable tanks with rubber inflatable bombs. Sometimes they would move whole imaginary armies close to the enemy, with nothing to protect themselves but rubber artillery. Sometimes they would send Golyat Thornapple behind the enemy lines.

Golyat met many creative people who like him had been recruited into the Ghost Army—painters, designers, musicians, writers. In between working tricks on the enemy, hiding from bombs and bullets, and running for their lives, they talked about art. By the time the war ended, he knew what he wanted to do.

CHAPTER 52

Creeping Shrub

So Golyat, his tuition paid by the government under the GI Bill, enrolled in the prestigious Creeping Shrub Academy of Art in New Jersey. He studied drawing, painting, and the history of art. Golyat liked being an art student. He had his own little room, three meals a day, hot showers whenever he wanted, plus nobody was shooting at him. The teachers were nice to him, and he had a girlfriend named Blossom, who was large and round, his favorite shape for a girl.

Golyat worked hard, and showed talent. He did a lot of drawing and painting. He bought a 1938 Plymouth coupe with lots of rust, and he and Blossom would drive around the countryside in New Jersey, sketching and painting landscapes. But Golyat found it all a little unsatisfying. After designing fake farms, and hoping to design a fake village, and after arranging battalions of rubber tank after tank, truck after truck, and hundreds of dummy soldiers to be dropped by parachute, just drawing on a piece of paper or painting on a stretched canvas didn't amount to the kind of scale he wanted.

In the library of the Creeping Shrub Academy of Art, Golyat found books about murals. He studied these over and over. He found murals exciting. He began looking around for walls. He persuaded a local farmer to let him paint the side of his barn. Golyat painted a farm, like the one he had hoped to design in the war. It was a beautiful farm. The farmer was not happy with the painting because it made his actual farm look crummy by comparison. Golyat was not happy with the painting because he felt the barn was not big enough.

Golyat's senior project at Creeping Shrub was a set of designs and plans for a mural to be painted on Boulder Dam. The mural was to depict the history of westward expansion, the local Indian tribes, historical personages who had been in the neighborhood such as Mark Twain, Kit Carson, the marine hero Ira Hayes,

and also cowboys, prostitutes, Chinese railroad labor-
ers, Thomas Edison and Nikolai Tesla, the develop-
ment of hydroelectric power, Presidents Hoover and
Roosevelt, desert plants and animals, and a tribute to
the nation of Mexico and the Catholic church. After
he graduated, he sent the project as a proposal to the
Boulder Dam Commission, the States of Nevada and
Arizona, the United States government, the president
of Mexico, General Electric, the Ford Foundation, and
the Vatican, hoping to have it approved and funded so
he could paint it. Nothing came of this.

     He then went to Spain, with a plan to muralize
the medieval walls around the city of Avila. However,
he had been misinformed by Eddie Balchowsky and
did not know that the fascist-supported side had won
the civil war, and the dictator, General Franco, would
not be likely to approve his mural—but to be fair, the
other side would not have approved it either, since
the walls of Avila were about a thousand years old,
and in perfect condition—and pretty much anybody
who wasn't Golyat would have thought putting paint
on them would be a bad idea. Plus, it was pretty much
the same as his plan for Boulder Dam, and the con-
tents and persons depicted would not have meant
much in Spain.

     Golyat went back to Chicago and prepared a

brand-new plan, this time for a mural to be painted on the Great Wall of China. It would show the history of the planet, from the beginning of time to the present, and he included a large section about the life and deeds of Mao Tse Tung, thinking this would get the new Chinese government to consider his proposal favorably. I don't think he really believed he had much of a chance, and worked at the same time on a smaller project to be painted on the Pyramid of Cheops in Egypt. He sent both ideas off, and never heard back.

He then settled down to doing paintings on canvas, but he was dissatisfied and bitter. I asked him why he didn't try for some local walls, in churches, post offices, lobbies of new apartment buildings— things like that.

"Not interested," he said.

"So you never did any murals?"

"The mistake Michelangelo and all those other mural painters made was working too small. Do it right, which means do it big, or don't do it at all. I still remember how let down I felt after I did that barn."

CHAPTER 53

1947

Captain Shmendy

Of course, I continued to drop in on Arnold Zwieback's drawing classes. On one particular occasion the model was Captain Shmendy, a retired Great Lakes sailorman. Captain Shmendy wore a posing pouch, which is sort of like a bikini bottom and looks ridiculous, also one of those yachting caps. He had a great many tattoos on his wrinkled old hide, including some of lizards in ballet shoes and tutus—the same subject as some of Golyat Thornapple's paintings. There was also a tattoo of what looked very much like the white house with the vast interior where I had my little studio space in which I never did any work.

I was certainly curious about why those particular images, and was trying to decide whether it was good manners to ask a naked old person about his tattoos during the break.

It turned out I didn't have to ask. When we took a break, Captain Shmendy did not cover up with a robe like the female models did—instead, he held forth with a lecture about his life and career, pointing out the skin art related to different parts of his story. The lizards, he explained, he'd had done when the *ballet de reptile* from some island or other came to Chicago in 1939. The house I thought I recognized he claimed was the house he had grown up in, in Oshkosh, Wisconsin. These tattoos were on the captain's upper arms. Down one side of his body were portraits of the five women he'd been married to. On the other side was a list of sandwiches he had specially enjoyed, and the date on which he had eaten them—for example, in 1947 he had a fried egg on toast, which he felt deserved to be commemorated. I wanted to know if the lizards had anything to do with Thornapple's paintings, or maybe if Thornapple himself had drawn them, but it turned out to be impossible to ask the captain any questions. He was a nonstop talker.

Across his back was tattooed DEEP WATER WALLAH over an American eagle, and an old-fashioned sailing ship.

"This modeling is only a temporary gig," Captain

Shmendy said. "I'm expecting to be put in charge of an important expedition in the near future." Then, for some reason, he looked directly at me when he said, "And we'll be wanting some able-bodied young chaps to man the oars."

Needless to say, the guy was hard to draw, and all the students were frustrated. Except Billy Zwieback—he was sketching away energetically with an intent expression. I leaned over to get a look at his drawings—he was creating a cartoon character of Captain Shmendy, and had even designed a title logo, "Naked Old Loony." I could see why he was excited. It definitely had possibilities.

CHAPTER 54

She Knows Things

I was in the Art Institute, looking at *The Bedroom*, a swell painting by Vincent Van Gogh, when Molly found me. She had the Wolluf with her.

"How come they let you bring a dog in here?" I asked her.

"Because he's the Wolluf. He's not a dog. Anyway, I've been looking for you. Do you know a guy named Geets?"

"Sure, I know Geets. He's probably my best friend. He hasn't been around for a while. Did you see him?"

"He's mishi-gazu."

"What's that?"

"It's a Zen term. Can't be explained."

"So where did you see him?"

"He's at the house."

"The house where we hang out?"

"There."

"Now?"

"Now."

"Well, let's go see him."

"All right, but I warn you, he's tzu-mishi-wa."

"Zen term?

"Yes."

"Can't be explained?"

"No."

We were walking. "How did you know I knew Geets? Did he mention me?"

"No. He just set up a little workshop at the house and started working on his . . . work."

"And you came looking for me."

"Right."

"Why? Why did you come looking for me?"

"Because you're a friend of Geets, and I thought you would like to see him."

"But he never mentioned me."

"I said that."

"So why?"

"Why what?"

"Why did you know I was a friend of his?"

"How many times do I have to tell you? I'm studying to be a wise woman. I know things."

CHAPTER 55

He Bends Spoons

Geets had set up a little space in the weird house. His equipment consisted of a wooden stool and a small crate full of spoons. I could see why Molly thought he was tzu-mishi-wa—he was sitting on the stool, holding a spoon in his hand, and staring at it with an intense expression. He was so focused on the spoon that he didn't notice me until I was standing right beside him and spoke to him.

"Bushman lives," I said.

Geets looked up slowly. "You know, he literally does."

"So what are you doing?"

"I'm trying to bend this spoon."

"By staring at it?"

"Well, by directing the power of my mind at it. So how have you been?"

"Pretty well. I'm doing art. How about you?"

"I've had adventures and learned things."

"What did you mean, 'he literally does'? Who does?"

"Bushman. One day, Harold, you and I are going to see Bushman in person."

"Huh? You mean when we die?"

"No, see him—on Skolnick Island. He is like a king there."

"You know he is dead and stuffed and on display in the Field Museum of Natural History, to their shame."

"That is a mannequin covered in fun fur, part of the deception to cover the real shame—that of the Zoological Society and the city of Chicago in general, that he did not die, but simply busted out and went they know not where."

"But you know where."

"So I believe."

"Skolnick Island?"

"Yes."

"What is this Skolnick Island? I never heard of it."

"There are any number of things you have never heard of, my friend. Skolnick Island is named for Father Skolnick, a Jesuit who came over with Marquette and that crowd, and was an early explorer and naturalist. He was interested in gorillas. Before coming to North America, he was in Sierra Leone in Africa. Some say he collected a few particularly promising ones and brought them to Illinois with him."

Molly was standing a little way off.

"Mishi-gazu," she said.

CHAPTER 56

When Your Friend Is Nuts

What do you do when your friend goes nuts? Molly said she could probably cure him with mint tea—that having been the method used to cure her. I took this with a grain of salt, since it was fairly likely she was still crazy as a bat—I give the example of her insistence that the Wolluf, who was furry and four-legged and licked his own genitals, was not a dog but something else. And, as I thought about it, Geets, with his habit of climbing buildings, had probably always been crazy and this was just a new aspect of it. Well, I liked them both—and they were no crazier than a lot of people I knew.

"When do you think you'll be done bending that spoon?" I asked him.

"I'm about ready to take a break," Geets said. "I still have to get the hang of it."

"Why don't we all get a Greek salad, and then I'd like you to meet someone. I have a mentor. You want to come along and see him?"

"That's cool," Geets said.

CHAPTER 57

Just As Crazy

When we went up to Golyat Thornapple's place, he had photos and sketches of some kind of odd-looking building all over.

"My new project," he said.

"What is it?"

"Well, these are pictures of the Potala Palace in Tibet, the ancient residence of the Dalai Lama. I'm using them to begin planning a mural."

"You're going to muralize the Potala Palace in Tibet?"

"Something very like it, only bigger, and nearer."

"The invisible island in Lake Michigan!" Molly said.

"Skolnick Island!" Geets said.

"You know about Skolnick Island?"

"I know."

"It's invisible?" I asked.

"It's camouflaged! It's painted to look like water —it can be done, you know."

"And they have a Potala?"

"Very similar."

"And they are going to let you paint it?"

"It's being arranged. The Wolluf has been over there representing me."

"Molly's dog? The Wolluf?"

"He's not a dog. He's the Wolluf. Anyway, he's my agent."

So here it was: I had gotten a real, honest-to-goodness mentor and guide, and what happens? He turns out to be just as crazy as everybody else.

CHAPTER 58

Lake Scouts

Geets and I met at the outdoor café at the Nor-Well Drug Company for a cup of coffee and a blueberry muffin. I was sketching a couple of nautical types who were sitting at the other table getting doughnut crumbs on themselves. They were about our age, and wore blue sailor suits—like the kid on the Cracker Jack box. They must have had them since they were a lot younger, because they had outgrown them. Fat ankles and fat, hairy wrists stuck out of the cuffs, and the blouses were tight across the belly. Both of these tars were tall and fat, with close-cropped thick black hair, nerd glasses, and those Dixie cup sailor hats. I was having fun drawing them—they looked like wild boars stuffed into uniforms, and the little insignias and bo'suns whistles on lanyards were interesting.

"Those are not regular sailors," Geets said.

"They're not regular humans, as far as I can tell," I said. "But how do you know? They look like sailors to me—sloppy sailors, but what else could they be?"

"I was in the actual navy for a short time," Geets said. "Those uniforms are way out of date."

"You were in the navy? When was that?"

"Last month, it was," Geets said.

It had been just over a month since I had seen Geets last— and that was how long I had been doing the drawing thing. It seemed longer. "You were in the navy, and now you're not? What happened?"

"The navy decided that it would be better if I finished high school," Geets said.

"They kicked you out?"

"Entry-level separation. I can reenlist anytime after I graduate."

Sometimes you mean to say something and what comes out is not what you meant to say but what you were actually thinking. "What are you?" I asked the sailor boys.

"We're Lake Scouts."

"Is that like the Sea Scouts?" I asked.

"Nah. The Sea Scouts is connected to the Boy Scouts of America. They're all about water safety and boating technique—boring stuff."

"And what are the Lake Scouts about?"

"Well, it's similar, only we're more like vikings or pirates."

"Vikings."

"We have a lot of fun. We learn to tie nautical knots, and sing chanteys, study the great seafaring traditions—flogging, keelhauling, walking the plank, tattoos. Maybe you'd like to join the Lake Scouts."

"That should be a breeze for you, Geets, since you were an actual sailor."

"Recruit. But I know all the knots and some of the other stuff."

"We're actually going to go out on the water in the near future," the Lake Scouts said.

"Where do you have your meetings?" Geets asked.

"The basement of the Bahamian Rite church on Sedgewick," the scouts said. "Wednesday nights."

"I'll make a note."

CHAPTER 59

An Ancient Tribe

Wednesday night, Geets and I were sitting on a low wall across the street from the Bahamian Rite church.

"Are you seriously thinking about joining the Lake Scouts?" I asked Geets.

"I just want to see them," Geets said. "Look! They're starting to arrive."

All the Lake Scouts appeared to be tall and fat, pale-skinned and hairy, with the same short haircuts, and eyeglasses.

"That's interesting," Geets said.

"What is?"

"They all resemble one another."

"They're all tall, fat, hairy boys with glasses—

probably from the west side. What's interesting about that?"

"I think they are of an ancient tribe."

"Jews?"

"More ancient."

"Egyptians?"

"Older than that."

"And that is interesting why?"

"Just is. I'm interested in anthropogeny—that's human evolution. I have come to believe there are more loose ends around than is generally believed—and we just might be looking at a bunch of Neanderthals or something similar."

"Neanderthals in Chicago."

"Yes. Does that seem so unlikely?"

"Now that I think of it, it would explain a lot."

CHAPTER 60

One Potato, Two Potato

Though Golyat Thornapple was crazy, his was a standard or acceptable level of craziness. He was still able to teach me all sorts of neat things.

"Ah, Harold, just in time! I'm going to teach you how to eat a baked potato."

"I already know how to eat a baked potato."

"Are you sure?"

Golyat flipped open the oven door of his little gas range and drew out two big russet potatoes.

"First, with a fork, we poke a line of holes along one side of the potato," he said. "Then, using thumb and index finger we squeeze the ends until the potato bursts open along the line of holes we've made.

Cutting into a baked potato with a knife is something horrible and against God and nature."

At my house, we always cut into the potato with a knife, slapped some butter on, a little salt, and that was the whole deal. I became interested in what Golyat Thornapple was saying and doing.

"Now butter, of course—then the salt and pepper, a dollop of sour cream . . . I shake some dried chives from a jar—fresh chopped would be better, of course—and here is your basic baked potato. Partake."

I partook. It was pretty good, worth paying attention to, and clearly better than baked potatoes as executed by my mother.

"Is this how you have them at home?" Thornapple asked me.

"No," I said with my mouth full. "This is better."

"In your future life, as it may come to you to prepare baked potatoes, would you say you are more apt to make them the way Mama made them, or this way?"

"This way, without question," I said, dripping some butter on myself.

"I point out, in passing, that there are many variations on what toppings you may employ—cheese, for one, crumbled bacon, caviar, even."

"Noted."

"Now, if a kindly mentor had not, out of the goodness of his heart, given you the very potato you are presently enjoying—but if you read about it in a book, would you be inclined to try this approach to the *Solanum tuberosum* or common spud as contrasted with whatever your well-meaning but unenlighted mother might do to them?"

"Oh, without question, I'd give this way a try."

"And now, I will relate the important thing. Are you ready?"

"Ready."

"I am unable to make a baked potato as good as one I can imagine."

"Yet this one is very good."

"It is, and I thank you for the compliment—but mark you, every time I bake them, and as good as they may be, there is an ideal in my mind that they do not match."

"And this is the important thing?"

"It is—because that is the reason some of us make art, and why all of us need it. Do you get it?"

"Almost."

"Fair enough."

CHAPTER 61

A Clean Girl

The people who attended Arnold Zwieback's life classes, male and female, were rumpled and scruffy, also bedraggled. They all appeared to have just gotten out of bed, having slept in their clothes. They looked depressed, and slouched as they stood around on the corner, smoking.

Except one. This was a girl who always arrived in a taxi. She always wore crisp, freshly ironed cotton dresses, and expensive-looking sandals. She had clean feet. She did not have charcoal dust or grunge under her fingernails, and she had a genuine leather portfolio to carry her drawings in. She smiled at everyone, and seemed happy. Naturally, everyone avoided eye contact with her, and more or less ignored her. Billy Zweiback told me her name was Miranda Sheldrake.

"You're Harold Knishke, aren't you?" Miranda Sheldrake asked me one day. What could I do but admit it? "Would you like to come to a party?" She tore a corner off a sheet of expensive drawing paper and wrote an address and apartment number on it. "It's tonight. Nine o'clock. I hope you'll come." Then she got into the taxi that had come for her, and was gone.

I was puzzled and bewildered. Why had Miranda Sheldrake, a clean, unnecessarily cheerful, and apparently rich girl, invited me to a party? And why did she know my name, even? Well, I had a suspicion about that. A lot of people knew my name in connection with the song about Old Harold Knishke, which sung by Blind Beet was pretty much completely unintelligible. What I had begun to suspect was that not only I, but everybody, had no idea what the song was about beyond that it was about someone called Harold Knishke. That time at the Ugly Mug, Jenny Thimble had introduced me as the genuine and authentic Harold Knishke, the one in the song. I thought it was just a goof, but all the people applauded. Could she have thought the song, the complete gibberish song sung by Blind Beet, was actually about me? Could

Miranda Sheldrake have wanted me at the party because I was a famous somebody with a song written about him? Or maybe she didn't even know about the song, just that Harold Knishke was some sort of celebrity? Or maybe she found me attractive—maybe my rakish and painterly appearance struck her as charming. I asked myself: If I were a girl, would I invite me to a party? The answer was yes, definitely.

I looked at the address on the scrap of expensive drawing paper. It was 860 North Lake Shore Drive. It was in one of those two famous buildings designed by Mies van der Rohe, the ones that were perfectly rectangular, like a kid had made them with his Erector set, and they were supposed to be the most advanced and modern buildings ever built, and represented the future of architecture, and charged the highest rents in the city of Chicago. I was interested in seeing what the inside of one of those buildings was like. I had seen them from the outside, and they were fairly neat, I suppose. I mean, they were sort of . . . stark. They just stood there, glaring at you, and seemed to say, "I am a building. Kiss my ass." This was cool, as long as all the other buildings near them were the more old-fashioned type. The stark, squared-off buildings with no decoration of any kind made the other buildings look a little foolish, like they were overdressed. But there were a few other square slab buildings going up here and there in the city—apparently it was economical to build them like that. I wondered how cool the Mies van der Rohe ones would look when all around them were other big tall boxes.

CHAPTER 62

I Meet a Third

It turned out that it wasn't Miranda Sheldrake's party. It was at the apartment of a kid named Cordwainer Fish III on the twenty-third floor. Cordwainer the Third's parents weren't home. The rooms were spacious and had a nice feel to them, and there was an incredible view of the city. It so happened I had recently spent some time looking at the African collection at the Art Institute, so I was able to note that the Fishes' private African art collection had a lot of pieces that looked just as good to me as the ones in the museum. All the furniture had been designed by Mies van der Rohe himself, and I had the idea that the carpets were worth a lot.

I saw Miranda Sheldrake when I came in, and she saw me. She flashed me a bright smile and came over and kissed me on the cheek. She smelled pretty good. Then she took me by the hand and led me over to meet Cordwainer Fish III. "Cord, this is Harold Knishke," she said. She emphasized the word *this*.

Cordwainer Three was the most relaxed person I had ever seen. He was leaning against a sort of big rectangular thing that was the base for a Nimba headdress of the Baga tribe in Guinea. I knew what it was because the Art Institute had one. The Fishes had two—there was another one on the other side of the room—and they were both bigger and had fancier carving than the one in the Art Institute. Then I remembered that the African art collection at the Art Institute was called the Fish Collection. The Third was wearing a blue dress shirt with the sleeves rolled up, blue jeans, and loafers without any socks. He smelled better than Miranda, and from farther away.

"Pleasure to meet you, old chap," Cordwainer said. "May I offer you a martini?"

"Did you call me 'old chap'?"

"Yes. It's an expression of friendliness. I might have called you 'old chum.'"

"You might have called me 'old chum'?"

A martini is a drink served in a little stemmed glass, and it has an olive in it. I should have asked for a beer.

Most of the other boys at the party all looked more or less exactly like Cordwainer. The girls were like Miranda, who kissed various people on the cheek, not just me. The exceptions were one black person, one homosexual person, one sloppy, unshaven rude person, and me. It was a clean, relaxed, good-smelling crowd with white teeth and excellent haircuts. There was jazz playing on an excellent stereo system, and the place was air conditioned.

It turned out that everybody there, except for the exceptions, went to private schools—Bateman, Parker, the Latin School—and they were all going to go to Harvard and Yale. They all knew each other, and they talked to each other about other private school people they all knew who were not at the party. It was a lousy party.

The black guy and the homosexual guy were standing in a corner talking to each other. I was standing in another corner talking to the sloppy, unshaven rude guy.

He was pretty interesting. He was a sculptor. His name was Julius Hargrove.

"I haven't seen you at one of these before," Julius Hargrove said. "What are you, the celebrity?"

"I think I am. I mean, they think I am. It's because my name is Harold Knishke."

"Oh, like in the song," Hargrove said. "I'm the genius. I get invited so I can insult people and get drunk."

He liked martinis.

"Also, there is some pretty good nosh. Little cheesy things, or sandwiches usually. I think we're getting beef stroganoff at this one pretty soon. I prefer hors d'oeuvres because I can stuff tons of them in my pockets, which they love for me to do, and I can eat for two days off one of these parties."

The black guy and the gay guy in the other corner had quit talking to each other and were gazing off into space with bored expressions.

"Excuse me a moment," Julius Hargrove said. "I ought to do my thing." He spun around and shouted into the room, "Fucking nitwit capitalists! Pea-brained imbeciles! You're all dead, and you don't know it!" People tittered. Then he turned back to me, "That's all there is to it. Painfully easy, really."

"What's the point?" I asked. "I mean, why have us here? Nobody is talking to us."

"It's so when they tell each other about the party, they can mention we were here, and not just people they see every day, or people exactly like the people they see every day. They don't talk to us because they have absolutely nothing to say and couldn't possibly understand or be interested in anything we might say since we don't know the people they know. If you listen in on their conversations, you'll hear that all they can do is mention the names of people like themselves who are not present."

I listened. I learned that Freddie was in Palm Springs, and Buffy was in Rome.

"So, they really are dead and don't know it," I said.

"Afraid so," Julius Hargrove said.

CHAPTER 63

It's a Date

I was surprised and confused when Miranda Sheldrake hooked her arm through mine and told me she was ready to go. That she said this while gently tugging me toward the door could mean nothing but that she intended me to go with her. Julius Hargrove processed this even faster than I did.

"What? You're going already?"

"The evening is young," Miranda Sheldrake said. "We have places to go."

"You're going before the main nosh? What about the stroganoff?"

We were outside the apartment, waiting for the elevator.

"I told Cordwainer goodbye for both of us," Miranda said.

I was still processing. Apparently I was Miranda Sheldrake's date. If I had more social experience, I might have suspected this from her having invited me to the party. As it was, I had no idea what any of this meant, or how I was supposed to behave. We got onto the elevator.

"What is beef stroganoff, exactly?" I asked Miranda.

"It's cubed filet mignon sauteed in a sour cream sauce with onions and mushrooms, and served over noodles."

"And we're leaving before it's served because . . . ?"

"Because who wants to stand around eating at some dopey party with a bunch of teenagers when we can have much more fun?"

"Sour cream sauce?"

Outside in the street, she asked me, "Where's your car?"

"Don't have a car."

"No car?"

"Also, I don't know how to drive."

"Well, we can take a taxi."

"Don't have any money."

"You know how to hail a cab?"

"Actually, I've never done it, but it seems fairly straightforward."

"Some boyfriend material you are."

Boyfriend? I stepped out into the street and waved down a cab. We got in. Miranda told the driver to take us to the Bogenswerfer Gallery. "We're going to an art gallery at night?"

"It's an opening," Miranda said.

"What's that?"

"When they open a new show, they have a reception. You may still get your beef stroganoff, or anyway something nice, and you can meet important people."

CHAPTER 64

Minimonoism

The crowd at the Bogenswerfer Gallery smelled like the crowd at Cordwainer Fish III's party. They were not drinking martinis—instead, some kind of white wine that had a slight kerosene taste was being handed around in plastic glasses. It was noisy, people were laughing too loud. Everybody had fancy clothes.

The party was in honor of a painter named Lash O'Hara. There was a big piece of white cardboard on the wall with an explanation of the paintings printed in black letters. It seems that Lash O'Hara invented a kind of art called Minimonoism. Here's how it works—he paints everything in one color, say black. So a painting with the title *Sunrise in the Stockyards,* which was one of the paintings in the show, has the sky, clouds, animals, buildings, all painted in flat black. The effect is the same as if O'Hara had just taken a big brush and painted the whole canvas black. But that would not be Minimonoism. In fact, he had carefully painted the whole scene in realistic colors, and then had carefully overpainted the whole scene, stroke for stroke, in black. If anyone purchased the painting (and several of them had little red stickers on them, which Miranda Sheldrake explained meant they had been sold), they would get, in addition to the painting, an x-ray film showing the underpainting— and the x ray was painted over with the same color as the painting—in this case flat black. It would be possible for the owner of the painting to chip the flat black paint off the x-ray and see the picture of sunrise in the stockyards, but of course that would diminish the value of the artwork, which was in the thousands.

Also on the wall there were blowups of reviews of Lash O'Hara's work from various newspapers. All the reviews said he was a genius. And, of course, there were the paintings, all of a single color. They had titles like *Nude Eating a Pizza, Storm over Lake Michigan,* and *Lincoln Park—Blizzard.* That one was all white.

Lash O'Hara was also on display. He was wearing a gray suit, shoes, socks, shirt, and a hat, all the exact same color—and he had makeup of the same color on his hands and face. There was a little knot of people standing around him, and he was explaining Minimonoism to them—saying more or less the same thing that was on the poster. He also was telling them that Monominimalism, apparently another variety of painting, was not the same as Minimonoism and was someone's attempt to steal his idea.

"Is this a goof or a stunt of some kind?" I whispered to Miranda Sheldrake.

"Are you kidding?" she said. "This gallery sold a hundred thousand dollars' worth of his paintings last year."

Girls in black and white uniforms carried around trays with miniature hot dogs with cheese and a strip of bacon wrapped around them and fastened with a toothpick, as well as the kerosene-tasting wine. The hot dogs were not too bad, and I ate quite a few of them.

CHAPTER 65

Meet the Boss

"Come meet Lydia Bogenswerfer," Miranda said.

Lydia Bogenswerfer was wearing boots and a lot of makeup. She was smoking a black cigarette in a long holder. "Who have we here?" she asked, and smiled in a way that struck me as a little creepy.

"This is Harold Knishke," Miranda said. "He is really talented."

"A young Turk, eh?" Lydia Bogenswerfer said. "Are you at the Art Institute?"

"I've been studying with Arnold Zwieback and Golyat Thornapple," I said.

"Impressive," Lydia Bogenswerfer said.

She thinks Arnold Zwieback and Golyat Thornapple are impressive?

"Bring some of your work around to the gallery. It's possible I can do something with you." She waved the cigarette holder in such a way that I knew she was done talking to me.

Miranda steered me away. "That went really well," she said. "Don't say I never did anything for you."

"I would never say that," I said. "You invited me to Cordwainer Fish III's party and you brought me here—in a taxi—and I have never had little hot dogs like that before."

"Most important, I introduced you to Lydia. She obviously liked you. She can give you a career."

"A career?"

"Yes."

"Well, that would be good, I guess."

"Now I'm curious. I'd like to see some of your work."

"You've seen my drawings at the life class," I said.

"I don't think I ever noticed. Do you have a studio or someplace you keep the stuff?"

"I do, in fact. It's not far from here. You could come over sometime."

"Could we go now?"

CHAPTER 66

The Art Business

As we were leaving, Julius Hargrove was coming in. "You left before the stroganoff," he said. "That was a rookie move. It was excellent."

"It's little hot dogs here," I said, "with bacon and toothpicks."

"Oh, good! Pocketable!" Julius Hargrove said.

"Did you ever consider lining your pockets with plastic freezer bags?" I asked.

"Way ahead of you, buddy."

Outside in the street, Miranda said, "Rats! I don't see any taxis."

"It's not far at all," I said. "We can walk."

"Really?"

As we walked, Miranda explained the art business to me.

"Let's say someone like Lydia Bogenswerfer likes you," she said. "She might put some of your work in a group show and see what kind of reaction it gets. Of course, if someone buys it, you get a third, and if it looks like a lot of people are interested, she might give you a contract."

"What kind of contract?"

"You get a certain amount every week, say a hundred dollars, and she pays for your art supplies. In return for this, anything you draw or paint for let's say five years belongs to her."

"And if she sells anything, I get a third."

"No, because she has been paying you that hundred dollars, and paying for your canvases and paint and so forth. You don't get anything. But she will give you advice, and tell you what to paint and how to paint it."

"She tells people what to paint?"

"Sure. Who do you think told Lash O'Hara to invent Minimonoism?"

"Lydia Bogenswerfer?"

"I'm sure she did."

"But Minimonoism is all idea. Anybody could do the paintings—they're all one color."

"What's your point?"

"My point is, anybody could do the paintings."

"Wrong. Only a Monominimist could do them, and actually only Lash O'Hara, because so far he is the only one."

"And he gets a hundred dollars a week, and free paint?"

"I would think he gets more. He's a top artist."

"And Lash O'Hara, and presumably other artists . . . they all do what Lydia Bogenswerfer tells them?"

"A stable. It's called a stable of artists. They have to. It's a contract."

"A stable, like horses? That doesn't sound so good to me."

"It's good. It's the way you get to be a famous artist."

"What if you didn't care about being a famous artist?"

"Who doesn't care about that?"

"Do you want to be a famous artist?"

"Sure, or just famous—it wouldn't have to be as an artist."

"So why don't you show Lydia Bogenswerfer your art, and maybe get her to give you a contract?"

"I think she only likes boy artists. Which, come to think of it, I do too."

And then, Miranda Sheldrake took hold of my shoulders, turned me around, and smooched me. It took me completely by surprise. Except for some fairly dismal experiments when I was a lot younger, I had never had a full-on lip lock—and Miranda clearly knew what she was doing. It was interesting how my brain completely stopped working—that is, it was interesting thinking back on it, when my brain started to work again.

It was just about this time when we arrived at the weird white house. The lizardy ragamuffins were at work, getting in some night whitewashing, and who should be standing in the street in front of the house but Molly?

"Who's this?" Molly asked.

"This is Miranda. I'm taking her in to see my drawings."

"Like fun you are." And then, to Miranda, "Push off, girlie."

"What?" Miranda asked.

"Sling your hook. Fade. Disappear."

Then the Wolluf rose up from the bushes and did not so much snarl or growl as smile at Miranda. I imagined I heard him say—or maybe he really did say . . . in English . . . "She wants you to go away. I think you should."

We could hear Miranda's tiny sandals clicking rapidly on the pavement after she had disappeared into the darkness.

"What was the idea of that?" I asked Molly.

"You can't just bring people in here."

"You brought me in."

"That's different. You belong here. You're an artist."

"How do you know she isn't an artist?"

"Is she?"

"She might be."

Molly stared at me.

"Anyway, she smooched me. I was thinking she might do it again."

"Don't let your lips lead your life, pal," Molly said. "By the way, be here tomorrow morning—I'm taking you to meet someone."

CHAPTER 67

Late Movie

My father was up, watching the late movie, when I came home.

"*King Kong,*" he said. "Ever see this movie?"

"Parts of it," I said.

"It's a sad and disappointing movie on so many levels," he said.

"I just thought it was dumb."

"It's that, too. It was a big sensation because of the special effects, which were advanced for its time. But all the characters have bad motives, and it's full of racism. The most sympathetic character is the ape, who is himself sort of an idiot—but more likable than the humans. So how is your art career coming along?"

"Funny you should put it like that."

"Oh?"

"Well, I never actually gave any thought to it being a career—I mean, I have just been enjoying learning to draw, and going around drawing stuff. But tonight someone took me to an art gallery and I found out a few things about the business."

"What did you find out?"

"Well, it's sad and disappointing on many levels."

"Careers can be like that," my father said. "If you're thinking about a job, I repeat, you can't do better than work for the Salami Council. If you'd like to enter a profession, I suggest you think about medicine, law, or accountancy. You could also go out west and work on a ranch, if that appeals to you, or be a dentist. But if you want to do art, you ought to do it as an art and not worry too much about how it's used to make money."

We watched the movie for a while. King Kong, who did not strike me as such a great special effect, had square teeth like a human instead of gorilla-looking teeth. For some reason, I found this embarrassing.

"I think I'll go to bed," I said.

"Good night, son," my father said.

CHAPTER 68

Three Dimensions

Who should Molly take me to meet the next morning but the sculptor Julius Hargrove? He had a place in a cobblestone alley. It had obviously been a stable for horses. There was a wide door, wide enough to drive a carriage through, and above that a loft door with a wooden beam sticking out and a pulley on the end. That must have been for hoisting bales of hay. Molly put two fingers in her mouth and whistled loudly, and Hargrove appeared above us and slid down the rope attached to the pulley.

"This is Harold Knishke," Molly said. "He wants to help you."

"Ah! The guy from the party! You ever done any sculpture?" Julius asked me.

"No."

"Know anything about it?"

"Not really."

"But you have always wanted to do it."

"Well, I can say I haven't not wanted to do it."

"Are you willing to work for nothing?"

"Pretty much."

"Good. You are now my apprentice."

"Shouldn't I clear this with Golyat Thornapple?"

"I already did that," Molly said. "It's all right with him."

"Let's get to work," Julius said. "I have a big project going, and only a week to finish it. The other apprentices are in there."

I went through the stable doors. In a large room, four tall, fat, pale, spiky-haired, bespectacled guys— Lake Scouts—were hacking at a gigantic hunk of wood.

Julius Hargrove put an odd-looking tool in my hand. It was a little like a hatchet and a little like a hoe, with a slightly curved blade.

"This is an adze," Julius said. "It's sharp, so make a point of not driving it into your calf or knocking off any fingers. As you see, I have marked off sections of this gigantic hunk of wood with my Flo-Master marking pen. What you apprentices have to do is whack away the markings. As you do this, I will come around with the Flo-Master and mark more. Once we get past the adzing phase, you will learn the handling of gouges and chisels for the finer carving. Lunch is at noon—it's little hot dogs wrapped in bacon, and cheap wine today. Be happy in your work."

The hunk of wood was obviously a section of trunk from some really huge and ancient tree. The Lake Scouts had taken off their sailor blouses and were working in their T-shirts, chipping away where Julius had Flo-Mastered cross-hatching on the wood. As they chipped, they sang radio commercial jingles.

> *Any time of the year, it's the beer of good cheer*
> *Drink Canadian Ace, Drink Canadian*
>   *Aeeeece!*

> *Drink Edelweis, it tastes so nice*
> *It tastes so nice, drink Edelweis*

> *Ticonderoga, has won its way to fame*
> *It's a great American pencil, with a great*
>   *American name*

Pepsi-Cola hits the spot
Twelve full ounces, that's a lot
Nickel, nickel, nickel, nickel . . .

They didn't converse, or respond to anything I said to them. They just sang the jingles under their breath, and adzed. These guys all looked exactly alike, so much so that I wondered if they were identical quadruplets . . . or maybe not regular human beings. And of course there was Geets's theory that they were Neanderthals. It crossed my mind that they might have been some sort of robot—but how would such a thing be possible?

CHAPTER 69

What Is It?

When we broke for lunch and were sitting around eating the somewhat stale tiny hot dogs and drinking the cheap wine, which was more disgusting at room temperature than it had been at the art gallery, and tasted slightly of plastic—evidently Julius had poured it into a freezer bag—I asked him what this thing we were carving was.

"Gorilla head," Julius Hargrove said. "It's a commission. Also, for some reason it's top secret. I was given a page of specs about what size, and how the back side of it should be carved. You'll notice, as we progress with it, that it doesn't have a base or a flat bottom so it can stand on its own. It's obviously intended to be attached to something. I wasn't given

any information about that, but it's my guess it's a figurehead for some kind of boat or ship."

"Who are you making it for?"

"I had to sign something promising I wouldn't
say," Julius said. "Not that I have any idea who the
person is, beyond the name on the check I was given."

"So, you got paid, and we . . ."

"You're getting lessons in basic techniques of
wood carving, and lunch, and I am not charging you
a cent."

CHAPTER 70

A Week of Sculpting

Lunch the next day, and for the rest of the week, was bologna on white, and room temperature Kool-Aid. I did learn a lot about handling carving tools, also these curvy rasps called rifflers. The thing got smaller, and smaller, and began to take the shape of a gorilla head. Julius would mark areas with his Flo-Master, and show us how to hold the tools, and which way to cut. As we got closer to the finished head, he did more and more of the carving and rasping himself. It was turning out to be a pretty good gorilla head, with a noble expression, and I was proud to have worked on it. I couldn't tell if the Lake Scouts were proud or not. I didn't have an actual conversation with any of them beyond exchanging a few words about how it was a warm day, and hand me that chisel please. They sang the radio jingles constantly. Toward the end, Julius gave us sandpaper and had us smooth certain areas.

We were allowed to cover it with a base coat of white lead paint. Julius painted it in gorilla colors— he did all that himself, and inserted glass eyes, which made it really lifelike. Then we gave the thing three coats of marine varnish, and it looked splendid.

I was only a little surprised when the two lizard-like, wrapped-head-to-toe types who whitewashed the weird house were on the truck that came for the head. All of us, the whitewashing guys, Julius, the Lake Scouts, and I, lifted it onto the truck and covered it with a tarpaulin. Then the truck rolled away, Julius gave each of us a pack of Picayune cigarettes and a bottle of Dad's Old-Fashioned Root Beer, and that was the end of my week as a sculptor's apprentice.

CHAPTER 71

So How Is It Done?

"I wonder if I could really be an artist."

"What makes you think you're not one now?" Golyat Thornapple asked.

"Well, I guess I am if just drawing stuff makes one an artist. But I think there's more to it."

"Like what?"

"Oh, like having an idea. Or being able to make stuff that . . . um . . . sort of organizes the way someone sees or thinks. It's like this—there is stuff in the Art Institute, starting with that painting by de Kooning, that, after I look at it, nothing is ever quite the same. It changes me. I think that's art, at least the possibility of something like that happening."

"Well said. Of course, not all art has to rock your

world and make you a different person, not in a big way, necessarily—but I would agree it ought to have a heartbeat, and not be just lines or dabs of color on a surface."

"So how do you get to be someone who can do that, or how would you know if you have a heartbeat?"

"Everyone has a heartbeat."

"You know what I mean. So far I've learned something about how to draw, and a little about color— and I just spent a week helping to make a piece of sculpture —but those are just skills."

"Skills are important."

"Sure, but how about the other thing? Are you just born with it, and some people have it and some people don't, or can you develop it?"

"It's my opinion that everyone is born with it to some extent, but you still have to develop it."

"Well, that's my question. How do you do that?"

"You live."

"You live?"

"Yep."

"So, let's say I want to be an artist, a real one. I try to learn all the skills and technical stuff, and for the rest I just kick around, living, and maybe the heartbeat thing kicks in, and maybe it doesn't?"

"Pretty much—but I'd add that there's a difference between just living and educating yourself."

"Finally we're getting somewhere. Educating yourself—like going to schools and colleges?"

"Some do it that way. You could also consider seeking special experiences, like going to Tahiti."

"Like Gaugin did!"

"Right, or observing the horrors of war."

"Like Goya!"

"Or going on a whaling voyage."

"Who did that?"

"Herman Melville."

"He wasn't a painter. He wrote *Moby-Dick*."

"Same difference. But taking a trip by water and seeing some strange and exotic place might be useful to someone considering becoming a painter—you ought to try that."

"If I ever get the chance."

"Chances come along a lot more often than you might suppose."

CHAPTER 72

Did You Get One?

"**D**id you get one of these?" I asked Geets.

"I was just going to ask you the same thing," Geets said. "Did you sign me up for the Lake Scouts?"

"I did no such thing. Did you sign me up for the Lake Scouts?"

"No, I did not. But this thing came for a parental signature. It gives permission for me to attend the Lake Scouts summer camp and cruise. It came to my grandmother. And she signed it."

"My father signed the one that came to him. I know nothing about a summer camp and cruise."

"Nor do I."

"How did the Lake Scouts even know our names or where we lived?"

"No idea."

"This is weird."

"It is. It's weird."

"You told me there were Lake Scouts working for that sculptor guy. Could they have signed you up?"

"They hardly talked to me. We never even exchanged names. Mostly they sang old radio commercials. Besides, why would they know your name, let alone your address?"

"Do you think it could be something sinister? We could be abducted, and our families wouldn't look for us because having signed these things they would assume we were off with the Lake Scouts."

"Who would want to abduct us, and why?"

"I can't think of a single reason."

"Me neither. I'm throwing mine away."

"So am I."

And we forgot all about it.

Just a Beatnik

I ran into Miranda Sheldrake walking arm in arm with Billy Zwieback. They were gazing at one another with happy, goofy expressions.

"Billy is my boyfriend," Miranda said. "He is getting a one-man show at the Bogenswerfer. And you are just a beatnik."

"Dig," I said. "Man."

Look!

Geets showed me a spoon. It was bent.

"I finally did it!" he said.

"You bent this spoon?"

"I bent it!"

"With the power of your mind."

"Yes!"

"You didn't help it with your fingers a little?"

"Not a bit!"

"Well, that is pretty impressive."

Geets smiled broadly. "Bushman lives," he said.

CHAPTER 75

Let's Go

I must have been asleep for an hour or two. I woke up sensing there was someone in my room.

"Geets?"

"No, it's Molly," Molly said.

"Molly?"

"What? Do I mumble? I said it was me."

"What are you doing in a young man's boudoir in the middle of the night, and how did you get in here?"

"It's all right, we're not alone. The Wolluf is here too."

I switched on the light. There they both were. I smelled bananas on their breath.

"I brought you a banana."

"Thanks."

"Eat it and get dressed. We have to go someplace."

"Where to this time?"

"A guy named Glugo has built a scale model of a Roman trireme—that's a kind of ship."

"I know what a trireme is. Ancient ship. They had three rows of oars on each side, and so what?"

"It's authentic in every detail."

"Good for Glugo. Maybe he will win a prize from the model builders club."

"It's fully functional."

"Whoop-de-doo." I was yawning.

"It's a three-quarters scale model."

"Huh?"

"It's eighty feet long. They're launching it in Belmont Harbor in about an hour."

"I bet this thing has a gorilla figurehead."

"I believe it does."

"Okay, you've got my interest. Let's go."

"Get dressed and do whatever, and make it fast. We'll sneak out of the apartment and meet you downstairs."

"So, you won't be climbing out the window."

"Oh, and leave a note for your parents say-

ing you're going to be at Lake Scouts camp for a few
days. You might want to grab a change of clothes, and
maybe a sweater."

"What? What?"

"Hurry up. You don't want to miss this."

CHAPTER 76

Nosy Parker

We were making our way through the park in the darkness. I could hear distant thunder. No, it was too regular for thunder. *Boom boom boom*. It sounded like a bass drum, only deeper and probably louder when you got close to it.

"What's that?" I asked Molly.

"Drum."

"I assume Geets figures into this business . . ."

"He does."

". . . because we both got these Lake Scouts permission forms for our parents to sign. Are we in the Lake Scouts now?"

"What's with all the questions all of a sudden?

Up to now you've just done what I tell you, as you should."

"I got nosy all of a sudden. So are we Lake Scouts?"

"Of course not. There's no such thing as the Lake Scouts."

"Oh? And what about all these tall, pale, fat, identical-looking . . . ?"

As we passed under a streetlight I caught a glimpse of Molly's don't-be-stupid expression.

"Are they robots?"

"Not exactly."

"Are they zombies?"

"Not exactly."

"Well, what are they, exactly?"

"Questions, questions. If you wanted to know all this stuff, why didn't you ask me when we weren't busy?"

"I'm asking now."

"You'll have plenty of time to ask your questions when you get to the island."

"This is Skolnick Island we're talking about?"

"Sure."

"And I'm going there?"

"Not if you don't want to. But you'd be a fool."

"Look, who's in charge of all this stuff that's been going on? It's you, isn't it?"

"Me? I'm not even from around here. I'm from upstate New York."

I was getting confused. Confused and impatient. "Wait . . ."

"No time to wait. Look! It's in the water already!"

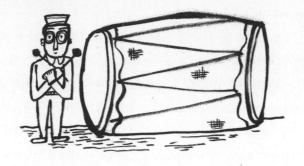

CHAPTER 77

It's in the Water

There was a frantic scene at Belmont Harbor, which is where people keep their pleasure boats. They looked tiny compared to the *Father Skolnick Maru*—that was the name painted on the prow. The drumming had stopped. I saw the drum, a huge thing, like a barrel on its side. It had a skin on each end. I guessed it had been beaten to keep time as the *Father Skolnick Maru* was carried to the water. There were enough Lake Scouts to have done it. I saw some of them gathering up lengths of thick rope and piling them on a flatbed truck, which I supposed had brought the boat to the harbor. More Lake Scouts were carrying things onto and off the boat, hauling on ropes, fiddling with oars, holding torches so others could see, rushing in all directions—it was organized chaos.

The trireme itself was incredible. It was like a rowboat crossed with a centipede. There was the gorilla-head figurehead, and there must have been fifty oars on each side. Except for the oars, there was nothing about it that would make sense as a boat to a modern person. It reminded me of some kind of prehistoric animal at the Museum of Natural History. It was floating lightly, dwarfing the little sailboats and cabin cruisers.

I could tell which was Glugo, the guy who had built the thing. He was a King Kong–looking type in a leather apron, gazing with love on his creation. Golyat Thornapple was standing with him, a bundle of papers rolled up under his arm. And Captain Shmendy, nude with the posing pouch and the yachting cap, was running around on deck, testing ropes and hollering orders. Of course he was going to be the captain on this trip—who else?

Geets turned up. He introduced me to a guy, built along the same lines as Glugo, named Sterling Hugebee. "I understand you are going to take part in the rowing along with Geets here," Sterling Hugebee said.

"Me? Row? This triple-decker? It looks sort of complicated."

"You're a husky youngster. "I'll bet you can pull with the best of them. Besides, named Harold Knishke as you are, don't you want to do like the hero in the song?"

"Harold Knishke in the song rows a boat?"

"I thought all you kids knew that song."

"It's time we got aboard," Geets said.

"It's time we got aboard," I said to Molly, who was standing nearby.

"Time you did. I'm not setting foot."

"You're not coming to the island?"

"I'll see you there, but I'm not going by water. I'm allergic to boat trips since I took a ride on the Hudson one time."

"How are you going to get there?" I asked.

"Let's go," Geets said. "Captain Shmendy is going to instruct the crew."

CHAPTER 78

Aboard

Complicated did not begin to describe what it was like on board the *Father Skolnik Maru*. First we had to walk on a gangplank that was a long, bendy board about six inches wide, as the boat bobbed in the water. Once we were on deck, everything was crowded and difficult, and there were about a hundred large, clumsy Lake Scouts milling around and tripping on things. A couple of times I was almost knocked overboard.

Finally Geets and I got into place to row. There were little narrow hard benches, offset and stacked three high, and the oars were of three different lengths, the longest at the top, then shorter, then shortest. The way things were set up, if you were not at the top—I was at the bottom—the oar of the rower above you could smack you in the face if you were not leaning back and pulling when he was.

It was about a hundred rowers, one to an oar, and except for Geets and me, all of them were Lake Scouts. I hoped they knew what they were doing—I certainly didn't. Geets didn't seem bothered by any of this, I supposed because he had been in the navy for a little while and that built his confidence. But I was pretty certain they hadn't given him trireme-rowing training.

Golyat was on deck—he was a passenger and wasn't going to row. Geets's friend Hugebee was on-shore with Glugo, the boat builder. And I thought I saw my father! But I was peering out of the oar hole and couldn't get a good view. Victor was with us, and also the two weird whitewashers—they had brought a drum onboard, a smaller version of the giant one. Obviously they were going to tap out a rhythm for us to row to.

Victor poked his face down into the little cramped space. "Hey, kids! Glad you made it! I've been wanting to take this trip back to the island for most of my life!" He was all excited.

"Say, Victor—about this island . . ." I started to ask, but then Captain Shmendy started to holler and everyone got quiet and listened.

"Crew! We're about to get under way. The tricky part of this voyage will be getting the craft out of the harbor. There are lots of small craft at anchor, and we will have to thread our way among them and sink as few as possible. Listen to my commands, and obey instantly."

Geets was sitting in front of me. "What commands? How do we know what to do?" I whispered to him.

"Just do what the others do," Geets said. "How difficult could it be?"

Incredibly difficult is how it was. Fortunately, the Lake Scouts all moved as one person, and by simply freakishly panicking and scrambling to do what they were doing while actually whining with fear, I was able not to get my oar tangled up with the oars of the rowers before and behind and above me.

This is what Captain Shmendy said, one command after another, without stopping:

"Prepare to give way! Give way together! Easy, starboard! Easy, port. Easy, easy, port! Back, starboard! Hold water, port! Blades up! Blades down! Lay on your oars! Belay that command! Hale up the brails!

Helm's-a-lee! Handsomely now! Hold water, all! Sharp, starboard! Forge ahead!"

I have to hand it to those robot zombie Neanderthal or whatever they were Lake Scouts. I had no idea what they were doing, but they did what they did the moment Captain Shmendy hollered a command, and they all did it together. I was sweating and whimpering and going insane, but I managed to move my oar more or less where they moved theirs and just a little after.

It took at least an hour—maybe two.

CHAPTER 79

A Calm Lake
and a Prosperous Voyage

And then, Captain Shmendy hollered, "We've cleared the harbor! Now give way together, cheerly! And strike up a chantey!"

It was straight rowing now. The lizardly white-washers kept a steady beat on the drum. A lake breeze cooled our faces. The rosy-fingered dawn had begun to illuminate the surface of Lake Michigan, and we sang,

> *Row, row, row your boat*
> *Gently down the stream*
> *Merrily, merrily, merrily, merrily*
> *Life is but a dream*